DRAGON'S REIGN: THE WHITE DRAGON REVEALED

(GAY DRAGON SHIFTER ROMANCE)

DRAGON'S REIGN

BOOK FIVE

X ARATARE

INTRODUCTION

As the other Dragon Kings and Queens arrive in Reach, Caden realizes that keeping his identity a secret from the clever and powerful royals will be impossible. But who does he reveal himself to first? It will *not* be Illarion…

But Caden isn't the only one who reveals themselves. An enemy drops their disguise…

PURR

*V*alerius picked Caden up into his arms. The young man let out a delighted "whoop". Caden wrapped his arms around Valerius' neck.

"Where are we going?" Caden asked.

Had the young man not understood that Valerius intended to make love to him here? In his tower? In his bed? He tipped his chin up to indicate where they were headed.

"I like cool sheets against my bare skin. Don't you?" Valerius challenged.

Color flooded Caden's cheeks. "Oh, most definitely."

The earlier "whoop" was repeated several times as he raced them from platform to platform that curled along the outside wall of the tower. They passed by a platform solely for his clothes. Caden reached over as they went by to finger the leather and silk he had teased Valerius about earlier, even as he himself wore it with such evident pleasure.

"Look at all those boots!" Caden chuckled. "I love the fur trim, though those look almost like something Illarion would wear."

"The gods forbid!" Valerius laughed.

He thought of his fellow Dragon Shifters and Illarion's comments about him seducing Iolaire right from under their noses. Illarion was right, of course even though he had not made his intentions towards Caden clear, at least not in words.

It is because my seduction of Caden is not the reason he is uninterested in them. He has all his friends and family here.

But was that true?

They reached the topmost eyrie where he had one of his beds. There were two. One on the ground floor of the tower where Chione had discovered him, which was heavily curtained and tucked away from the world. That was the one where he could avoid sunlight and could cocoon away from the world. But this one, the one he took Caden to, was fully open to the air.

It was a custom-made mattress, twice the size of a standard king, with a simple platform frame of maple. The bedding was whites and soft grays like the first touch of twilight. It reminded him of sleeping in the sky on a mountain. He set Caden down on the cool bedding. Immediately, the young man stretched out, his arms nowhere near able to touch the edges. Caden closed his eyes and let out a contented sigh.

"Oh, man, this is niiiiiccccceeeee," Caden dragged out the last word. "I don't think I ever want to leave."

I may not let you. You look so right here in my bed, Caden.

He winced a little. He really did sound like one of those actors in the Werewolf mate romances. He smirked then as he realized how very jealous the Werewolves would be to know he had a mate.

The very thought came unbidden and naturally. But it had him freezing. He immediately looked at Raziel, to see what his Spirit would say in response to that. But Raziel said nothing. Because Raziel was asleep. But just like him, Raziel was not sleeping alone.

In all his years, he had never seen anything quite like this. There was still a separation, a hazy line, but he could see *both* Raziel and Iolaire. They were curled up asleep, but their foreheads were practically touching. Iolaire's much smaller head was pillowed on one claw while Raziel's claws were outstretched towards the White Dragon Spirit as if wanting to hold onto Iolaire. He thought about telling

Caden about it, but he decided not to. How would Caden react to their Spirits loving each other like this. And that's what it was. His grouchy, fiery Raziel had never looked so at peace or content before. But now…

"Valerius?" Caden had cracked open his eyelids in the midst of him frisking against the cool sheets.

He snapped out of his shock. "Y-yes, my Caden."

"*My* Caden?" Caden twinkled at him.

Valerius decided that action rather than words would serve him better. He was a man of few words after all. But his actions were legendary. So he launched himself on top of Caden. Caden's reaction was perfect. His mouth opened in an "O" of shock and he closed his eyes tightly as Valerius pounced on him. He landed though on his hands and knees so he didn't actually land on the young man. He lowered his face so that he was half an inch from Caden's. The young man opened his eyes again to peer up at him.

"Meep?" Caden asked.

Valerius grinned and kissed Caden's nose this time. "Meep indeed."

Caden broke into laughter and wrapped his arms around his neck once more. Time seemed to stretch and elongate until it was like a ribbon of silk rolling into an unfathomable distance. This was what eternity was like and he felt it with Caden. To go along this path together and not alone…

Wasn't that what Caden had offered him earlier? The young man showed a deeper understanding of his feelings at twenty-five than he had known countless times that number. Even until Caden said it, he had not truly quantified and explored what he felt, especially since taking over rulership of this world. But Caden had put it neatly and easily into words. He smiled down at the young man. It wasn't a bright and happy smile, but more a tender one. Caden's eyes widened in wonder.

Yet Valerius knew something was troubling Caden that was, not necessarily greater than Serai's death, but was striking at the core of the young man. Caden had no poker face. Even when he smiled and laughed, if something was bothering him, it showed in his eyes. And it was there now, along with a great deal of desire and impishness.

"Are you happy?" Valerius found himself asking.

Caden's eyes went wide again and he answered rather breathlessly, "Y-yeah. Of course!"

"Even with all the burdens put upon you?" Valerius searched his face.

Caden tightened his arms around Valerius' neck. "Yeah, because I have... I have you."

Valerius' throat tightened to the point where words were simply not possible. He leaned down and kissed Caden fiercely until they both needed to breathe.

"You know, I'm really excited for us to make love, because the way you kiss just blows me away," Caden murmured.

Valerius chuckled, his voice restored. "What about my actions by the pond? Are those not as memorable?"

Caden's pupils grew larger and his lips parted as his breathing increased. "Uhm, that was completely unforgettable. But I think your kisses tell me more."

Valerius carded his hands through Caden's short hair, playing with the silky strands. Caden pushed up against his touch. "Do they?"

"You kiss me like you mean it," Caden explained.

Valerius saw Raziel's head moving closer to Iolaire's. That hazy line grew a little hazier.

"I do mean it."

But what did he mean? Were they talking about the same thing? When he wasn't letting himself think, he seemed to know exactly where he wanted to go. There was no doubt. But then he would remind himself of Caden's youth and inexperience, about how it was a huge commitment for both of them, for what it would mean in terms of what happened next. He could not do casual with Caden, which was an answer in and of itself, because he had always been casual with everyone else.

Caden stroked his cheek. "I'm losing you again."

"Never." His treacherous mouth had no sense. He should be reeling this back. Making it light and airy, as if they were just going to enjoy each other's bodies and nothing more!

Caden's hands moved from his neck and cheek to his shirt. The young man stuck his tongue out of the side of his mouth as he concentrated on undoing the buttons. It was adorable. Valerius could not help running his thumb along Caden's bottom lip. Caden grinned, but didn't stop unbuttoning his shirt.

Valerius studied that beautiful face. Caden was beautiful, but it was his sense of humor, kindness, enthusiasm for life over all that made him so attractive. Valerius traced those lovely features with his fingertips. He felt a whoosh of cool air as Caden pulled the tails of his shirt out and then urged him to lift one hand and then the other so the shirt could be shucked off and tossed to the side. Caden's hands fell to the fastenings of his leather pants.

"Shouldn't you take your shirt off?" Valerius lifted his right eyebrow.

"I have no pants."

Caden cheekily lifted the silk shirt up to his stomach, showing his lovely cock and balls and flat stomach. Valerius' stomach rumbled with hunger again. He remembered Caden's taste and he wanted that earthy cum on his tongue once more.

"If you were a Werewolf, I would think you wanted to eat me up just like Little Red Riding Hood." Caden waggled his eyebrows.

Valerius' voice dropped low and smoky, "Wolves have nothing on Dragons."

Caden drew in a deep breath and his cock stirred. "Oh, really?"

"I shall have to show you. To demonstrate."

Valerius then ripped open the shirt of his that Caden wore. Caden let out a startled laugh.

"I was sort of hoping to save this shirt," Caden teased him even as he stretched deliciously beneath Valerius.

"I have plenty of others just like that one."

But Valerius would keep this ruined shirt. He'd put it in a chest and take it out to remember this night and Caden. He really was just like those lovesick wolves!

As he gazed down hungrily at Caden's golden skin—with a swath of white across his groin—he felt his own cock swelling in the prison of his pants. But he didn't want to undo them just yet. He wanted to extend this almost painful anticipation. Caden reached out and put a hand on the bulge of his cock. He let out a grunt in appreciation as Caden cupped him.

"God, I forgot how huge you are." With a swallow, Caden looked around for something. A frown on his pretty lips was followed with, "You have lube right? I'm never going to get this monster inside of me without it."

Valerius snapped out of his almost daze of lust. He shook himself. "I do… but not here. I've never had sex with anyone here."

Caden blinked at him. "You haven't?"

"No. This is my private space."

"But you're letting me be here. Making love here. Sleeping here?" Caden made the last sound almost like a question. As if he would kick Caden out after being done with him!

He cupped the young man's face. "Yes, sleep here, love here, be here." He kissed Caden's nose to lessen the impact of those words. He didn't want Caden running. Then he was getting up from the bed.

"What—where are you going?" Caden squawked, his hands questing for Valerius, but just missing him.

"To get lubricant. My monster wants to find its home in your body," Valerius said, knowing it was cheesy, but saying it anyway.

He had just spun on his heel to run down to the platform where his bath was when Caden called out his name, "Valerius!"

Valerius spun around. Caden was up on his knees. The ripped shirt fluttered open, showing all of his loveliness. Valerius' breath caught and his cock throbbed. If he wasn't careful, he could cum just at the thought of Caden.

How long has it been since I've felt this? Never. I've never felt this.

"Valerius," Caden repeated and he nervously licked his lips, and Valerius thought he wouldn't say what he intended, but would make a light-hearted comment instead. Yet Caden pressed on, "It's not for me either."

Frowning, as he was unclear on Caden's meaning, Valerius asked, "Not what?"

"Casual," Caden said after a moment's hesitation. "It's not casual for me. This." He gestured between them. "It's like those movies for me."

Valerius took two long strides back to the bed. He caught Caden's chin and kissed him hard and fiercely to try and imprint what he felt in that touch of lips. When he pulled back, Valerius' throat was tight as he took in Caden's beautiful hazy look of happiness, but he managed to get out, "They should be writing movies about us. They will be."

Caden let out a breathy laugh. "Yeah, because Dragons are so much better."

"Because what we have is real."

Then without waiting to see what Caden's reaction was, he went to get the lube.

⸻

Caden watched as Valerius jogged down the steps to where a shower and bath just stood out in the open. Not that he was looking at the shiny chrome or sleek fixtures—though he definitely wanted to bathe there—but instead he was gazing at Valerius.

Real? This is real. And not casual!

The thought that maybe Valerius was only with him because he was the ninth Dragon Shifter tried to intrude on his good thoughts. Valerius liked him. Maybe more than liked him. Letting him take all these liberties, opening his private lair, protecting Caden… these were all things that showed so much more of what Valerius felt more than words ever would. He'd dated guys who could talk up a storm with wild proclamations of love, but Valerius could hardly open his mouth without tripping on his tongue when he spoke of emotional things.

Valerius had opened a cabinet, and in his haste and eagerness to get back to Caden, he was simply tossing things over his shoulder. Some of them landed on the broad stone landing, but many more tumbled into space and landed on the ground floor of the tower far below. Caden's cheeks hurt, he was smiling so broadly. He had Valerius *eager*! Valerius was so experienced with sex, that Caden had no hope that he wouldn't find things with him a little pedestrian, but Valerius seemed as excited as he was.

Caden looked down at his cock. It was already flushed pink and leaking. He could feel his heartbeat in it. He could cum any second, especially if he kept looking at Valerius' muscular ass. He bit his lower lip, reached down, and squeezed the base of his cock until the urge to orgasm faded somewhat. Not entirely. Not even close. But he would be able to last at least until Valerius was fully seated inside of him.

He looked up to see Valerius again, assuming he would still be looking for lubricant, or walking up the stairs. But instead Valerius was right *there*. On the bed. Inches from him. Pants bulging with that barely contained cock. Caden let out a breath.

"How did you get up here so fast?" Caden gasped.

"Enthusiasm." Valerius cracked a grin, but he looked very determined.

A delightful shiver wound its way down Caden's spine. "Oh."

"Prepare yourself for me," Valerius commanded. His voice was soft, but Caden sprung into action as if he had been shouted at.

Valerius pressed the tube of lubricant into Caden's hands even as his eyes never left Caden's face. Caden found himself falling backwards and drawing his feet up towards his ass. He, too, didn't stop looking at Valerius. They were really doing this! He was actually with Valerius! In his bed! With him there!

And it's real! He's real. I'm real. This is real!

He could smell Valerius all around him and that scent made him both feel safe and utterly aroused. He knew Valerius would never hurt him, but there was still that lilt of danger like when one falls asleep with the warm glow of a fire on one's face, knowing there's a risk it could set the whole house on fire. Valerius was restrained power and danger with him.

Caden snapped open the bottle of lubricant. It made a shockingly loud *snap* as he did. He squeezed the bottle and a gush of lubricant filled his left palm. It was cool and he should have heated it between his hands, but he didn't.

With his eyes locked on Valerius, he slicked his fingers and immediately reached down between his legs. Valerius' heated gaze stayed on his face for a moment before following his hand. Caden wanted to give him a show, but his fingers felt clumsy as he sought his own opening.

Valerius' lips parted and with a grunt, suddenly, the Black Dragon King was swatting his hand out of the way and putting his *mouth* where Caden's fingers had been questing for. Caden had never been eaten out before. Valerius' clever tongue lapped over his hole and he let out a whine. The Dragon King put his hands on the underside of Caden's thighs and rolled him back to have more access. Then it was tongue and teeth and wetness and heat.

Valerius' tongue pushed inside of him and wriggled around. His teeth rasped almost decadently against the tender skin of his asshole. The heat of his mouth had Caden's back passage muscles easing, opening, yielding to that attack of desire.

Heat cascaded through Caden as Valerius *sucked* on his opening and then thrust that agile tongue in and out and in again. Caden smeared lubricant on those perfect wintery sheets as he clawed at them, trying to find an anchor in this storm of pleasure. Every single nerve ending he had seemed to be located inside of his ass. His cock just throbbed—another heart—with every thrust of that tongue inside of him. But it wasn't just his cock. His whole body was alight. Fireworks were going off in his blood and he was lightheaded.

Then Valerius had his hands and was reapplying lubricant to the fingers on Caden's right hand. Then he led Caden's hand to Caden's own opening. Caden already missed Valerius' tongue inside of him so he thrust his pointer finger inside of himself, simply not to feel empty. He moaned at the feeling of being pierced.

"Beautiful," Valerius whispered.

Caden's eyes snapped to the Black Dragon King. Valerius was staring at his ass and finger as if he were a starving man. Caden would feed him what he wanted. He pushed that finger inside of himself as far as it could go and lifted up his hips. He let breathy moans escape his lips. Valerius' hands dropped to his crotch and he pressed the palm of his right hand over that leather-clad bulge. His gaze did not leave Caden's ass.

Caden moved that finger in and out of him. He imagined it was Valerius' cock as he desperately moved his hips in a circle, trying to get more of Valerius—or rather his finger—inside of himself. But Valerius was much thicker. One finger was not enough. He was going to be pushed to the point of aching. He was going to feel every inch of Valerius' cock so he had to be prepared. He slipped a second finger inside. He scissored them apart. He heard Valerius' breath catch which just had him more desperate to show how much he wanted the Black Dragon King inside of him.

A third finger was thrust inside even though he wasn't quite ready for it. But the slight pain was good as it calmed the roiling volcano inside of him. He was surprised he hadn't cum already. His cock was a hot bar tapping against his stomach, spattering precum with every tap. But he wanted only for Valerius' pleasure at that moment.

He reached down with the lubricant and put the nozzle to his spread opening to send a gush of clear gel into his back passage, making himself slicker. And soon his three fingers were moving in and out of his body almost easily. Valerius' hands were suddenly scrabbling at his pants. His huge cock sprang out the moment the button and fly were undone. Caden's breath caught at the sheer size of him.

Big all over!

Caden bit his lower lip to stop from laughing. He'd seen Valerius' cock before, but now with it about to go inside of him, he realized even more just how impressive it truly was. He pulled his fingers out of his ass. There was a wet, smacking sound that was pure sex as he did so. And then he was squeezing more gel into both hands as he reached for Valerius' cock. He let out a whine as he touched that velvety flesh over the hard shaft. Valerius shuddered as his head fell back, eyes shut. Caden grinned.

But if Caden thought that Valerius would remain the one more undone, he was wrong.

In a swift, fluid movement, Valerius lifted Caden up onto his lap, his hole directly over the tip of that massive cock. Valerius' eyelids were cracked open and it looked like they were completely black. The pupils were blown wide by desire that there wasn't even a ring of iris to be seen.

And then that cockhead, as large as a piece of ripe fruit, was pressing against his stretched opening. Caden's hands, slick with lubricant, gripped Valerius' powerful shoulders as the Dragon King drew him down millimeter by inexorable millimeter onto that cock. The head was so thick but amazingly pushed inside, stretching his unruly opening that tried to close up, to not give him entrance.

Valerius' lips were against Caden's right ear. "I will not be denied."

Caden shivered and his ass muscles unclenched. He felt Valerius smile as the Black Dragon King dragged those lips down his throat, only to linger at where the shoulder and neck met. He bit the flesh there. His tongue came out immediately after to lick and sooth. But that pain distracted him from the pain of that final breach as Valerius' cockhead popped through and he opened fully for the Dragon King's use.

Valerius' hands on his hips were feather-light. Caden's thighs quivered; he simply wasn't able to hold himself up and instead sank down onto that hard rod of flesh that pierced him to his core. His ass cheeks settled against the tops of Valerius' still leather-clad thighs. The sensation of his bare flesh against Valerius' clothes was electric. His cock jerked even more so at that then the sensation of being filled.

We're connected! God, I can feel every inch of him!

They remained still. The thump of both their heartbeats could be felt where they were physically connected. Valerius' mouth found his and they were kissing. It was that kind of kissing that made Caden's toes tingle and his ass clench. Valerius grunted when his already tight back passage tightened further around his cock.

"Careful, I will cum," Valerius' voice was deep and raspy and skated along Caden's spine.

11

"That's sort of the idea," Caden said, his mouth against Valerius', breathing in the other man's breath.

Valerius grinned and then he was rolling them forward. Caden was on his back once more with Valerius on top of him. Caden's legs wrapped around Valerius' waist. This position caused Valerius' cock to sink even deeper inside, which Caden hadn't thought possible. He gasped and trembled at this feeling of being breached yet more. Valerius swallowed that gasp and took his breath away again.

As Valerius began to roll his hips forward, Caden remained still at first, but then he started what felt like a liquid glide between them. Caden's heels dug into Valerius' spine as he sought to keep that massive cock within him even as it started to move in and out. The feeling of friction was electric. Even the thin stream of pain around his opening had Caden's nerves sparking with pleasure. His cock was slapped between Valerius and his bellies. It was like one of those balls that was held by a string to a paddle. The sting of that was glorious and their bodies moved faster and faster.

Valerius' fingers dug into his hips as he ground his front against Caden's ass. Caden let out a cry that he simply couldn't keep in. He tipped his head back, lifting his throat towards Valerius as if he were one of those wolves submitting. Valerius' mouth was on his neck. Biting, kissing, licking, *claiming*.

Caden's hands raked down Valerius' chest, leaving red marks in his fingertips' wakes. They healed immediately and he did it again, wanting to leave some sign on the Black Dragon King's magnificent body that this had happened.

Valerius pistoned inside of him. Short, quick, powerful thrusts that had Caden's teeth rattling in his skull. But the pleasure... oh, the pleasure... was something that seemed to take over his entire body. He was just one living nerve ending. His whole body reacted to his oncoming orgasm.

He arched up. The tip of his head was the only thing touching the bed while he clenched his legs around Valerius' waist and his finger gripped the Dragon King's biceps. His mouth opened in a scream that Valerius caught with a kiss.

Valerius' hips slammed his front into Caden's ass and held it there. Caden felt Valerius' cock swelling even more inside of him. His own cock did the same. Caden would later swear that they came at the same moment. That their heartbeats synced up and then they both came. He felt the heat of Valerius' cum fill him even as his own painted their chests in ropy lines of pearlescent semen.

They held that pose for what seemed like forever as the cum spurted from both of their bodies, but as it stopped all the strength seemed to leave Caden's body. He slumped, but Valerius caught him and pulled him up into his arms. Valerius was holding him. The Black Dragon King was shaking. His lips moved against Caden's left shoulder. Kissing him and murmuring something in a language that Caden did not know. And as they caught their breath and aftershocks of their orgasms ran through them, Caden heard a familiar yet unfamiliar sound.

"Iolaire is... purring," Caden said, half laughing and half touched as his Spirit continued to sleep.

Valerius was silent for a moment and then in a tone that was almost reverent but definitely amused, "Raziel is, too."

A MATTER OF FAITH

"*I* think I could get used to this," Caden purred as Valerius washed his back.

"As could I," Valerius murmured.

Caden leaned his forearms against the still cool stone wall even as hot water and silky suds sluiced down his back, ass and legs. The back washing had really become a back rub. Caden really wanted it to change to another lovemaking session, but already they were cutting time short on Valerius getting onto his conference call with the President of the United States and the Prime Minister of Canada. They wanted an update on the White Dragon situation, all the other Dragon situations, and, of course, the bombing.

"You cannot put this off, Valerius," Chione's voice had risen up from the tablet that Valerius had blearily squinted at. She hadn't exactly woken them. The sunlight had slowly lifted the veil of sleep, but he and Valerius had remained cuddling in bed.

"Oh, yes, I can," Valerius grunted.

Chione actually laughed, before firming her tone, "All right then, you *shouldn't* put this off. How about that?"

"Why not? I am comfortable." Valerius leaned over and kissed Caden's bare left shoulder just out of Chione's vision, but she must have heard the sound. Her cheeks were suspiciously pink and a smile was playing around her lips when Caden looked over at the screen-- though she couldn't see him.

"I see that." That suspicious smile was growing as were the pink patches on her skin. "But I am sure that the comfort you feel now is but the beginning of many comfortable times ahead."

"I think she wants me to be a good influence on you and tell you to talk to the world leaders," Caden said even as he snuggled his head on Valerius' chest.

"That's exactly what I'm hoping," Chione raised her voice a little so she was certain that Caden had heard her.

Caden sighed. Valerius sighed. Chione rolled her eyes.

"It is very difficult being king," Valerius groused.

"I'm certain that Illarion or Mei or one of the others would be happy to relieve you of that burden, my king," Chione reminded him.

Valerius growled. Raziel--who Caden could still see in his mind's eye and who was still asleep--also growled and its legs twitched as if dreaming of hunting Illarion down and ripping off his wings. Iolaire just let out a soft whistle-snore.

"Arrange a call in…" Valerius pursed his lips. "An hour."

"Thirty minutes. You have a breakfast scheduled with the other Dragon Shifters in an hour," Chione countered.

"At least I'll have a reason to get off of the phone quickly." And Valerius had cut off the connection with Chione.

That was what had led them to the glorious open-air shower. With many kisses and fumbles they had somehow left the sanctuary of the rumpled bed, down the stairs and under the spray of a gigantic rain shower waterhead. There were sixteen jets that sent hot pulsing sprays on their fronts and sides. Caden felt like he was being embraced by hot water. Valerius' hands lingered on his ass.

"You have five minutes before you need to be on that call," Caden reminded him even as his cock quivered in front of him. All of this hot water and suds and touching was utterly maddening, but he was determined to be a *good* influence on Valerius. Too much was going on in the world for Valerius to be distracted.

15

"Hmmm," Valerius grunted, but he did slowly remove his hands from Caden after he finished washing Caden's back and ass.

Caden wilted at the loss of his touch. He turned around in the spray. He found himself touching Valerius, putting his hands on Valerius' chest. "How Werewolf-movie-corny is it to say I miss you already?"

Valerius tilted his head to the side with an amused smile on his lips. "If I tell you that I feel the same way perhaps it knocks out the corniness?"

Caden grinned, got onto his tiptoes, and kissed Valerius on the lips. Valerius turned off the sprays and they toweled each other off with thick, soft, fluffy towels before going to the racks and racks of Valerius' clothing. Since it was all black or white, Valerius did not even have to seemingly think as he randomly grabbed leather pants, thigh-high leather boots and one of his many armor pieces that covered his right arm, but left just as much skin exposed as covered.

A servant had gone to Caden's home to get a bag of his clothes that Tilly had put together for him. He was pleased to note that his sister had packed his favorite jeans with rips on the knees and a soft t-shirt with the name of a band that had long faded away with many wash-ings. She'd even managed to pack the pull-on gray sneakers he loved.

"What do you think about me telling Esme who I am while you are on that call?" Caden asked Valerius.

Valerius turned to face him, still slotting a buckle with a thoughtful expression. "She would be a good person to begin with."

"It would also show that you don't suspect her of being behind the bomb business. I mean I'm sure she knows that, but it would probably make her feel better." Caden shrugged.

His stomach felt a little lurchy about telling Esme who he was, but he was also excited about it too. He thought of talking to her, really talking to her, about the powers they had and loads of other things.

Valerius nodded as he cinched the buckle tight. "I think that is a good idea. She will likely have some ideas of how you might reveal yourself to the world with less interruption for everyone around you."

"Less destruction, you mean." Caden gave him a faint smile.

16

In the cold light of day, he'd realized his "plan" or rather lack thereof to just tell the world his secret was insane. He was, once again, reacting instead of planning, which likely just showed how wrong he was to be the ninth Dragon Shifter. One thing he realized was that this didn't just affect him. His family. His friends. There were actually way more people than just him that would be affected by him coming out, so to speak. He had to do it right.

Valerius cupped his face. "Caden, you are not destructive. You could never be. I said that last night and I meant it. I mean it now."

Caden nodded, but he thought, *How sure would you be of that if you knew I was picked by chance?*

He looked at the sleeping Iolaire. Part of him wanted to wake Iolaire and ask why it had made such a poor choice. Another part of him thought he would never ask. What was done was done. And he was afraid of what answer the White Dragon Spirit would give. He just couldn't imagine the answer being complimentary.

Valerius was frowning again as he looked carefully at Caden. "What are you thinking?"

"Just… feeling a little…" *unworthy*, but he said out loud, "hungry and nervous," Caden said.

"Well, I happen to know that Esme always has a huge breakfast with eggs, rashers of bacon, a variety of pastries and more," Valerius told him, the frown retreating slightly.

Caden brightened at the thought of pastries though he guessed he should be more interested in the eggs and bacon rather than what was the equivalent of dessert for breakfast. But still, the thought of chocolate-filled, buttery croissants and raspberry streusel and blueberry muffins with fresh-squeezed orange juice sounded brilliant about now.

"Esme's room is in the north tower," Valerius explained. He frowned again. "I wish I could take you."

"There's like one minute before your call." Caden tapped his wrist where a watch would have been if he had worn one. He got up and kissed Valerius again. "Don't worry. I'll find her!"

Caden gave Valerius a final wave as the Black Dragon King

prepared to answer the video call with two of the world's leaders. He sort of knew where Esme was. Or at least he thought he did. Ten stairways later, several dozen turns, and finally a lucky break where he simply wandered down a final hallway and caught sight of the two guards dressed in blue silk and silver framing a set of double doors did he realize he'd finally found the right place.

Caden lifted up a hand and smiled to show he was friendly even as the guards stiffened. He realized as one of them--a stern-faced woman with frost at her temples--stepped up in front of him that he had no way of proving who he was or why he should be allowed to see Dragon Queen Esme.

"Halt!" she shouted though he was only a foot away and could hear her quite well. He did halt though, more out of shock than anything else. "Who are you? And what business do you have with Queen Esme?"

"I... ah... we're friends?" He made that sound more like a question than an answer. Considering Serai had been a long standing friend, he doubted that these guards would let him pass just for that in any case.

The stern-faced woman looked sterner. "Who are you?" She repeated with more emphasis. One of her hands had dropped down to the sword--yes, that was a sword!--on her hip.

"I'm--I'm Caden and--and--"

"Skye, who is it at the door?" Esme's voice floated out of the opening set of doors.

Without taking her eyes off of him, Skye stated, "A stranger who claims to be your friend. But I've never seen him."

The doors opened wider and Esme stood there in a pair of white culottes and a blue pirate-like top. She appeared tired but looked at him curiously as, obviously, she had never seen him in this form either.

"Young man," she began, "today is not the day to look for autographs."

"Queen Esme, we *do* know one another. But you probably don't recognize me because I'm not wearing *all white*," Caden emphasized the White Dragon's coloring.

Esme froze a moment, thinking, then her expression cleared and she let out a delighted laugh as she realized what he was saying. "Oh, my goodness, forgive me for not recognizing you right away! Come in! Come in!"

He smiled and edged past Skye, who still looked at him with a furrowed brow and uncertain glances. Caden wasn't sure about her either and only breathed a sigh of relief when the doors were shut behind them.

The room they entered was breezy. Tons of sunlight splashed inside through the thrown open balcony folding doors. The opening to the balcony was over twenty-feet long and gentle breezes tinged with the scent of flowers flowed inside. There was a long dining room table on which were arranged computers, tablets and loose paper. Some photographs, countless documents and more in small neat piles were set before every space.

"Your war room?" Caden gestured to the table even as Esme just stared at him with open interest.

She half turned. "Oh, yes, that's all of the information I have on Serai. All of the ingoing and outgoing communications she made. Of course, she wasn't foolish enough to communicate directly with whoever she was working for on these. She undoubtedly had burner phones and other means of communication. But there will be clues here. I will sense something out of place. Eventually."

"If anyone can figure this out, it's you. Valerius says that you are the most intelligent of the Dragon Shifters," Caden said.

A mirthful glint entered her blue eyes. She took his hands in hers. They were soft and cool and there were several rings on them. A square-cut diamond, a round ruby and a rectangular emerald. They were all incredibly beautiful.

"How can Valerius know that unless he has plumbed all your depths?" Esme asked, and Caden's cheeks flooded with color at the use of the word "plumbed" though he didn't think Esme meant it sexually. "You are the White Dragon Shifter, yes?"

He nodded. "I'm Caden. Caden Bryce. You met Iolaire already."

She returned the nod and let out another delighted laugh. "My goodness, you are so *young*. And adorable! Such a handsome young man. I am going to take the grandmother's prerogative and pinch your cheeks."

She did just that which had him laughing and blushing for some reason. His grandparents had died when he was still in his early teens. So it felt nice having someone who would treat him like a grandson.

"Please sit down. Would you like something to eat or drink?" she asked.

His head was already bobbing. "Valerius said you like breakfast. I like breakfast. I mean I really like food of all kinds right now."

She laughed again. "Oh, yes, you must be starving. Well, you are in luck. I was about to have something out on the balcony. There is nothing more healing than morning light."

He followed her outside onto the balcony. He blinked as that golden light hit him. There were two tables on the balcony. One was a round table near the railing so that the diners could look out easily. Then was a larger table that was laden with food off to the side.

Baskets of pastries, platters of eggs, bacon, sausage, tomatoes and, yes, *beans*, were set out. Caden vaguely remembered that English people sometimes ate baked beans for breakfast. There were piles of plates and cutlery.

One of Esme's people was there filling up a plate for herself. It was Molly. Serai's friend. Her eyes widened upon seeing him. Her eyes grew even wider as she saw Esme pat his cheeks.

"Fill up a plate and we'll sit down over there and talk. I am quite honored that you came to me like this," Esme told him.

"I wanted to from the beginning, but I was afraid. I'm still afraid. Not of you, but... everything. All of this," Caden admitted.

She nodded as if this made a great deal of sense. "Considering how things started, I don't blame you. But food first. Food and sunlight make things clearer."

Caden did as she suggested and loaded up a plate high with food and then balanced two croissants on the top, one chocolate, one almond dusted with powdered sugar. Molly lingered, too, picking out her own food, her eyes darting to him, and then back to the dishes. She was clearly wondering who he was. She probably *guessed* who he must be, but neither he nor Esme enlightened her.

"Molly, would you mind eating elsewhere today? Caden and I need some private time," Esme said gently.

"Of course, my queen." Molly curtseyed and took her plate into the tower.

Esme and Caden sat at the round table. Looking over the side of the railing, Caden could see a huge swath of sky, but also the botanical gardens below that were in High Reach. That was where the delicious scent of flowers was coming from.

"Since Reach is not near the sea, Valerius always tries to make me feel at home by surrounding me with flowers. I have quite extensive gardens in all of my homes," Esme explained as she lightly buttered a slice of toast.

"He's thoughtful. You wouldn't think it because he's so gruff and glowering a lot of the time, but he really does care for the people who are close to him," Caden said as he went to studying his own plate and trying to figure out how to attack the mound of food he had piled on it.

Esme smiled. "If you already know that about him, you must be close indeed."

"Yeah, but there's so much more to know," Caden said, even as he smiled uncontrollably.

Just speaking of Valerius reminded him of their night together. He had never slept so well. In fact, he'd always had problems sleeping in the same bed as his boyfriend. He didn't like to be held. Too hot. Too confining. He couldn't breathe properly. But with Valerius that hadn't been a problem.

He'd tucked against the much larger body and somehow it had just been *right*. He'd fallen asleep in moments and hadn't woken up a sodden mess. Instead, coolness had seemed to flow all around them the entire night. He wondered if it was because of Iolaire's ice somehow.

"So what brings you here to me in this form? Why did you choose to reveal yourself to me... or am I the last to know?" Esme looked a little bleak when she said the last.

"You're the first Dragon Shifter to know, Queen Esme," he assured her, reaching over to cover one of her hands on the table with his own.

"Esme, please! I would not have any formality between us. When we first met, I felt I knew you well already. Perhaps it is because our gifts are similar. Water and ice," she explained.

"I felt the same way," Caden said. "And I hope that you might be willing to teach me how to use my powers better because of it." His forehead furrowed. "Not that I have anything to offer you in return--"

"Your friendship is enough!" She waved his concern away. Her confidence was seemingly restored. "Besides, you stopped Serai from harming so many people when I did not."

"Any ideas as to why she did it?" Caden asked. He had a feeling that Esme had not slept last night, but had ceaselessly gone through Serai's digital life.

Esme shook her head. "The only thing about Serai that was perhaps *different* was that she kept her Faith."

"She was a member of the Faith?" Caden asked. "Sorry, it's just that every congregation I've heard of has no Shifters. Which, if I think about it, is weird."

"It's not encouraged," Esme explained. "There is already too much inequality between humans and Shifters. Humans believe that the Spirits are divine beings and, therefore, Shifters are divine... Well, none of us thought it was a good idea if Shifters agreed with them. But Serai still attended services."

Caden chewed on his chocolate croissant which was just the perfect mixture of salty, sweet and buttery. "I guess I see what you mean."

"Serai did not believe she, herself, was divine or anything like that, but she did have a deep reverence for the Spirits themselves," Esme continued.

"But surely the Faith has nothing to do with the bombings!" Caden couldn't think of the people his mother brought to the house once in a while, or who sang and danced in white robes, as anything but harmless. They were sort of a joke in his mind.

Esme turned her incisive gaze upon him. "I am glad you think that, though not because it is true."

Caden blinked at her. "So you think the Faith has something to do with all the unrest?"

"There have been *incidents*." She looked grim. "We have kept them out of the news because there are fears that the incidents would spread. Though there is already an unofficial whisper of them over the internet, of course. It is impossible to block something completely nowadays. But we've made those people seem fringe."

Caden frowned. "What incidents?"

"As you, yourself, know Spirits often bond with their humans during a crisis. The bigger the crisis, the better the chance a Spirit will bond with someone. Like yourself when the bomb was set," Esme explained. "There have been members of the Faith who have tried to cause these crises in order to cause more Spirits to enter this world. They've done so with extreme violence."

A sinking feeling filled Caden. "Are you saying that Serai set that bomb because she *wanted* a Spirit to bond with someone to stop it?"

Esme gave him a dry smile. "Yes, Caden, that is one of the very things I fear."

CHANCE

"*How* is the White Dragon Shifter?" President Goodfellow asked.

She was leaning forward with her elbows resting on top of the Resolute Desk. Her gaze was so intense that he felt it through the video screen. On the split screen opposite her, Prime Minister Stanton also seemed to feel that intensity and blinked a few times, shifting behind his own desk. She had seen Caden. She likely knew he was the White Dragon Shifter.

The United States would have been searching every image posted on social media, so even though they did not have the video he had, they would eventually figure out the boy behind the Dragon. Everyone would eventually know. He had tried to convince himself that anonymity was possible for Caden, at least, for a time. But that was because he had not been born into this technological age.

"How are they fitting in?" President Goodfellow pressed.

"Iolaire is fitting in just fine," Valerius said.

Iolaire and Caden actually *were* doing well considering everything. He heard more than saw Chione shifting on the couch behind him. She was indicating to him her discomfort at this line of questioning. Since he had taken up to the very last minute with Caden before getting on this call, he hadn't had a chance to tell her that Caden wished to come out.

He glanced over her. She had on a bronze skirt and white billowy blouse. Her feet were tucked under her butt and she had her tablet out as always. Their gazes met. Hers was questioning. His was soothing. She frowned for a moment but then her expression cleared as she realized that, for some reason, he wasn't worried about this line of questioning. He then turned back to the world leaders.

"We are, of course, aware that Iolaire wishes to keep their identity a secret," Prime Minister Staton stated, clearing his throat. "But President Goodfellow and I believe that since they are in your territory-- our countries--that as a matter of national security we should know who they are."

"A matter of national security?" Valerius said this as if tasting it. It annoyed him and he began to pace, arms crossed at wrists behind his back.

Chione drew in a sharp breath. She opened her mouth to speak, to try and smooth things over--he knew what she was going to say--but he held up a hand. She would tell him that they did not mean to suggest that he could not protect them from another dragon. But that was what it sounded like to Raziel. The Black Dragon Spirit's claws dug into the ground of its lair.

Think us incapable of defending them, do they? Raziel hissed.

Be calm, Raziel. They just wish to know who Iolaire's human counterpart is, Valerius told his Spirit, even as his back was up too.

They think Iolaire would harm them or us? Bah! Iolaire is our...

And then his Spirit shut down so swiftly that Valerius thought their connection had been cut. Not that such a thing was possible, but Raziel was clamping its mental connection down so tightly that he couldn't hear a peep from it.

Our what, Raziel? Valerius asked with narrowed eyes.

Raziel lifted its massive chin. *Our... friend.*

It is indeed, but I do not think that is what you were going to say, Valerius replied mildly.

Raziel was a terrible liar. He thought he knew quite well what word Raziel was going to use: Iolaire is our *mate*. His heart beat like a drum in his chest. Caden was so young. It was too soon. It would mean that their lives and fates were intertwined. Maybe that was why Raziel would say nothing. His Spirit did not want to pressure him or Caden.

Valerius turned back to the president and prime minister. He held up a finger. "First, I will give you the benefit of the doubt that you are not suggesting that Raziel and I are incapable of protecting you from *any* threat."

The two world leaders stirred uncomfortably. The president sat up in her chair rather like a terrier. The prime minister then froze, one hand at the collar of his shirt.

"We did not mean to suggest–" Prime Minister Stanton began.

"No, you did not, because that would be insulting and *unwise*." Valerius' eyes narrowed at them both. "Raziel and I are quite capable of defeating any and all other Dragon Shifters."

"Even if they all attack?" President Goodfellow whispered.

"Even if they *all* attack. But they will not." Valerius' lips pressed together as smoke poured from Raziel's nostrils. "You need not concern yourself with those fears."

"And what of Iolaire? Do they intend to stay here? And how will that affect things?" President Goodfellow pressed on.

Valerius glanced at Chione. One of her delicate eyebrows was lifted. She had mentioned something to him about these very questions being things that the two world leaders would ask. Both of them were used to being in control. Or at least the illusion of it. Now, he had basically asked them to trust him. Humans never did fully trust Shifters.

Considering what Illarion is doing to his people and Mei's mechanical soldiers they have a right to be uneasy, Valerius thought.

"Iolaire will be staying. They want no part in ruling..." Even though Valerius adored Caden and Iolaire, the thought of sharing the rulership of territory was still not sitting well with him. It likely never would. "But they will, of course, in time want to have an impact."

"They already have." Prime Minister Stanton laughed lightly into his right palm.

Valerius gave him a thin smile. "Yes, they have."

"They are a great asset," President Goodfellow said, warming to the subject. "They are an ambassador of goodwill. Interest in Humans First has declined since they've come. And the politicians with sympathies in that line have had their legs cut out from under them."

Valerius had been mildly aware--Chione had been terribly aware--of how Iolaire's obvious people-pleasing manner, especially among children, had turned the conversation about "dangerous and aloof Shifters" on its head.

President Goodfellow leaned forward again. Her hands were clenched in front of her. "And that is the real reason we are concerned about Iolaire. Not concerned. We want to help them help everyone."

Valerius grunted even as he caught Chione's eyebrow raise. This was nothing less than what Caden's father and his firm wanted to do. Everyone wanted to control the White Dragon Shifter, use it for their purposes, make it their puppet. He would never allow that to happen, no matter if Caden's identity was out or not.

"And what makes you think they need your help?" Chione asked in her patient way that somehow was more cutting than his snarls.

President Goodfellow focused on the Sphinx Shifter. Her eyes flickered to Valerius and away. "From how they have been described, they seem *young* and inexperienced."

"As are all Shifters when they first bond, but their own kind educate them in the ways of things," Chione answered almost sweetly, and then her tone changed, "Humans do *not*."

The president's hands tightened in front of her. Her knuckles went white. "But Iolaire is not some regular Shifter! They represent so much more and if they are going to be in our territory--"

"*My* territory," Valerius corrected her.

"Isn't it *ours*, too?" Prime Minister Stanton looked gray and uneasy as he said it, but clearly this was something that the two of them had cooked up. He really shouldn't have left them alone to speculate.

"Shifters take care of Shifter business. Iolaire is a Shifter," Chione reminded them, repeating the line that was said over and over as if it had mystical power.

"But Iolaire is another Dragon," Valerius found himself saying quietly. "They are different as President Goodfellow said."

Chione's eyebrows rose, but not in annoyance, but rather surprise. He really should have delayed this call and talked with her first. He was never going to regret spending more time with Caden.

"I understand your concerns. This is your home. You represent the people within it. You get to speak to me when others cannot. You must raise your concerns," Valerius said, causing everyone on that call to look a little amazed and a little worried. He did not speak this way. He scoffed at such things. Explaining himself was often abhorrent to him, and at best, a bore. But not in this. "Iolaire is not someone to be feared. But they are also not someone you control. My territory is run by me. Solely. What role Iolaire will take on will be decided in time. Right now, they have more than enough on their plate."

That seemed to quiet everyone. None of them could deny that becoming the ninth Dragon Shifter after stopping a bombing was anything to sniff at.

"They have had their life turned upside down," Valerius continued, staring at each world leader in turn. "You had a chance to *choose* to go down the path of leadership. You could have remained an anonymous citizen of my territory. But you choose to serve. Iolaire did not. They choose to save people at the expense of themselves."

President Goodfellow's head lowered. The hectic color in her cheeks fading somewhat. Prime Minister Stanton played with a pen. Most politicians were unfeeling snakes, but not these two. Somehow this time around the people had actually been lucky to get two real people who cared.

"We want to help. It is not that we do not think you capable, King Valerius," Prime Minister Stanton said. "But it is, as you said, something they were not expecting or prepared for."

"We know that they want to go slowly, but the way the world is..." President Goodfellow squeezed the top of her nose. "The world may not allow that pace. And we want to assist in helping them take on that role of leadership, and, *yes,* we want them to keep that seeming love for humanity they have. A connection between Shifters and humans. Iolaire can be that."

Valerius understood this. He and the other Dragon Shifters were too old to be as connected to humanity as they once had been. And Caden had been born after the War. He had lived in this split world between humans and Shifters.

"I have heard your concerns and will think about them," Valerius offered.

It was but a small concession. Caden was not ready for this. It was too much to ask of him.

Iolaire is wise, Raziel muttered. Its head was resting on its claws. *These humans are too quick. They take but do not give.*

That is their nature, Raziel. Their lives are short and their sense of urgency is ever growing, he said.

Raziel closed its eyelids. *Iolaire is all that matters. Not these mortal beings.*

But Valerius could not altogether agree. And he doubted that Iolaire or Caden would think so either.

"Will we get to meet Iolaire anytime soon?" President Goodfellow looked rather anxious about that.

Valerius smiled. She was a fan. "Yes, of course. I will arrange some time *after* the Dragon Shifters have gone back to their territories."

"Any idea when that will be?" Prime Minister Stanton did not look like he expected a very hopeful answer.

Valerius' expression went tight. "As quickly as possible. Are we done? For I must--"

"One last thing, King Valerius." President Goodfellow raised her hand and he was not surprised. There was always one more thing. Her constituents should be thrilled with her. They were getting their vote's worth.

"What?" His voice was crisp.

"King Illarion... are you going to speak to him about conditions in his territory?" she asked.

He gritted his teeth. He had known she was going to ask this question. He'd had this absurd hope that he'd get away from this conversation without that being brought up.

"I have already explained that King Illarion will not listen to my words, but only my claws, and to go down that route would cause far more damage to humanity," he reminded her tightly.

"Maybe if it wasn't just you, but if you spoke with the other Dragon Shifters present they would agree with you and put pressure on him--"

"Peer pressure?" His left eyebrow lifted.

"Surely, even he could not ignore all of you!" President Goodfellow looked so earnest. But she always did.

"I am amazed by your continued belief in the ability for some people to feel shame," he responded dryly.

She reminded him of a Girl Scout, he realized. She was smart and desperately wanted to do the right thing. She was motivated by this desire to help. But her imagination about people was limited.

Before anyone could speak, Valerius grabbed the remote to end the call. "I have heard your words, I will consider all you have said. I will be in touch."

He ended the call. The two world leaders winked out of existence. His head fell back and he stared up at the ceiling. He let out a long breath.

"That could have gone worse, you know?" Chione told him with a lilt of laughter in her voice.

He rolled his head to the side to look at her. She looked rather impish. He scowled at her.

"How?" he growled.

"She could have shown up in *person* this morning." Chione set the tablet to the side. "That was her intent."

"WHAT?!"

"I talked her out of it. Obviously." She patted the air between them.

"All the Dragon Shifters are here! What did she intend to do? Go canvas them about her desire for a better Shifter-Human world?" he scoffed.

But Chione nodded. "I think she would love that opportunity."

"I bet she would."

He groaned and scrubbed the back of his neck. He tossed the remote down and sprawled on the couch opposite her. He thought of how he and Caden had cuddled here just last night. He wished Caden were there right at that moment. But he was talking to Esme. He wondered how that was going.

"She believes that the rightness of her arguments must be acknowledged. In some ways, it's such a pure position and it does work on people." Chione tapped her stylius against her lower lip.

"Just not Illarion." He sighed.

"Oh, he couldn't deny the truth of what she was saying. He just doesn't believe in the same things. He's not a normal person. Not even before he bonded with his Spirit, I'm guessing," Chione said.

"None of us were." Valerius shrugged. "There were so many more like him before. They come in different flavors now in this much safer world. But back in the day, we both ran into Illarions. Small men with big insecurities that took them out by hurting others."

"Yes." She sighed and wrapped her arms around herself, rubbing her arms. "He just got very lucky."

Valerius nodded. At the moment, Illarion seemed the least of his problems. His concern was fully for Caden. He had captured the world's imagination. He should have seen that.

"They're going to find out who Caden is," Chione said suddenly. He focused on her. She looked grim. "I know we promised Caden that we would keep his secret and give him a chance for a normal life. Or, at least, a chance to grow into this new one."

"Caden knows this. Mei saw him in the mirror," he told her.

"Oh, dear. That is unfortunate." She studied him closely. "You do not sound too upset though."

"It was inevitable. I have no doubt that Mei knew in advance who he was," Valerius answered her. "Caden realized afterwards that keeping his secret wasn't possible, and might not even be for the best for those he loves. He was ready to call a press conference."

31

"Without talking to his parents or Wally? They have to be brought here or somewhere safe! They'll be set upon by reporters like a horde of locusts!"

Chione sat up straighter as if ready to bolt out of the door to stop this from happening. She wasn't necessarily wrong to believe Caden was quite capable of going into Drago Strike Square and shifting in front of all and sundry.

"Do not worry. Caden knows that too. He is aware that he needs a plan," he told her.

She didn't completely relax. "And what is that plan?"

"He does not know yet. But he is willing to take advice from you, me, Wally, even his parents, if they are speaking to him," he sighed at the end.

This was not the time when Caden should be at odds with his parents. He needed support. But, then again, this break had to happen.

"That is something." She still didn't look sold on it. Caden and Iolaire were capable of almost anything. "Should he announce who he is with the other Dragon Shifters here? Or after they leave?"

That was the question.

They will come back to meet him as if they have not already, Raziel muttered without opening its eyes.

He tended to agree with that.

"They will be offended if he doesn't agree to meet them in his human form," Chione mused.

"He is meeting with Esme now. Hers is the only opinion I care for." He waved a hand through the air.

He felt tired already. Maybe he could convince Caden to come back and nap in the sun. That would be lovely. But Queen Kaila was to be there by noon and Queen Jahara by that evening, followed by the final Dragon Shifter, King Anwar. There was no time for naps. Unless they just ignored them all.

Chione brightened. "That is good! I do think that Esme needs some show of support after Serai." Her expression went dark again. "Serai... I can't believe it. She remained an adherent of the Faith, you know. Even after she bonded with her Spirit, she still believed in their goodness. So why would she do this?"

His jaw clenched. The thought of Serai made him want to send everyone packing again and bunker down with Caden.

"I suppose I should feel grateful that this violence is not solely coming from my own territory, but that just makes dealing with the situation that much more difficult," he told her.

She slid her legs off of the couch and rested her elbows on her knees, chewing on the end of the stylus. "If this violence were about Shifter rule then Serai is the most unlikely of adherents. Humans First then may not be behind this after all."

"Landry's brothers have been implicated though. And on the contrary, the fact that she was still in the Faith means that she still has a great affinity with humanity," he disagreed. "I wouldn't put it past Jasper Hawes to have sleeper cells in the Faith to snag people just like Serai who feel some injustice keenly."

"An injustice that would be served by a bomb? By the deaths of innocents?" She threw her hands up. "Acts like these are normally used to create terror. Do what we want or another bomb. But that's not happening here. No one has claimed it."

"Because it went wrong," Valerius theorized. "Instead of people dying, the ninth Dragon Shifter entered the world."

"Unless that was intended." Chione was frowning.

"No one could have known that would happen." Valerius shook his head. "Not even I knew there were other Dragon Spirits out there. And even if someone knew that there was the possibility of another such spirit, they could not have known that the Spirit would bond with anyone. Caden was there by chance."

"But the Spirit wasn't," Chione stated. "We have always theorized that Spirits watch us before they bond. They pick someone. You've told me so yourself about Raziel. So if somehow they knew where the Spirit was--"

"That's too--"

But their argument was cut short by a sharp knock on the door.

"Come in!" Valerius called as he saw it was Simi at the door on the tablet.

Simi came in, red-faced and sweating, as if he had been running. "Forgive this interruption, King Valerius, Chione, but that robot Queen Mei brought you? It's gone insane!"

SPOILS OF WAR

*T*here was a wild whoosh of air that flattened Caden's hair and nearly sent the toast flying. A huge Green Dragon's head was suddenly level with the balcony. Green smoke billowed around its jaws. Caden's lungs tightened and he knocked over his chair, striving to get away from the noxious fumes. Esme continued to sit at the table, sipping her tea, and staring straight ahead as if Illarion had not just gassed their breakfast.

Holding his throat and drawing in wheezing gasps, Caden was almost flattened by another burst of powerful wind as Illarion rose up in the air so that his clawed toes were hanging two dozen feet above them. Then Illarion transformed and he gracefully dropped to the balcony into what Caden thought of as a "superhero pose".

Caden was still hacking up a lung as Illarion got to his feet and grinned at Esme. He didn't spare one look at Caden, but Caden's heart was in his throat... as well as poison gas. But, evidently, being a Shifter meant he wouldn't be killed by it. But, as he leaned over and hacked some more, he thought he might drop a lung or two on the ground.

Iolaire covered its nose with its front claws and closed its eyes tightly. That was when Caden realized his eyes were stinging as if acid was flung in them. He let out a cry and dug his palms into his eyes. Finally, when the stinging eased, he drew his hands off his eyes and stared blearily at Illarion.

Totally nude and completely unashamed of it, Illarion strutted over to the seat that had been Caden's, righted the chair, and sat down in it. Still grinning, Illarion ate Caden's bacon, which just added insult to injury.

"Esme! What a glorious morning!" Illarion inhaled another piece of his bacon.

Esme continued to sip tea even as the green poisonous mist swirled around her before disappearing altogether. It was only then that Caden realized that Illarion was here with him. The Green Dragon King would realize at any second who Caden must be! Panic had him taking a step backwards. Could he somehow retreat before Illarion noticed him?

Illarion's hand shot out with the unused coffee cup that had been set out but Caden had not used it. He was not a coffee person. He thought of it as water gone wrong. He froze at Illarion's movement and was prepared for the Green Dragon King to crow at finding the elusive Iolaire!

Illarion waggled the coffee cup at him. "Fill this." He didn't even look at Caden as he moved the cup towards him. "Must I repeat myself? Fill this."

He doesn't know who I am. He thinks I'm a servant or something!

Caden tried not to feel offended. This was a good thing after all! Yet it just proved all the more that Illarion did not care about Iolaire.

Caden met Esme's eyes. She nodded her head almost imperceptibly. He trusted her judgment so he took Illarion's cup and went over to the buffet where there was a silver coffee urn.

"Two sugars and a splash--just a splash--of cream," Illarion ordered over his shoulder. "Your staff, Esme, is horrible. Though, I suppose, compared to dear Serai, this one must be a treasure!"

Caden gritted his teeth. But he looked over at Esme again. She gave him a meaningful look.

"My people serve *me* very well," Esme murmured.

Illarion's brow beetled. "How a person treats their guests must not be important in your territory then."

"Guests are treated exceptionally well. You, however, are *not* a guest," she remarked.

Illarion took a large bite of croissant and talking with his mouth full and gesturing around the space stated, "This is not your castle. It is Valerius'. This is his food and drink. So I am just taking my part of his largesse here rather than in my assigned space." He glared over his shoulder. "Speaking of drink, where is my coffee?!"

"Coming," Caden grunted.

His hand hovered over the sugar bowl, considering dumping in as much sugar as the coffee could dissolve, but then he realized the goal was not to draw attention to himself. While the plan was to reveal himself, it wasn't to do so to Illarion. Not yet. Not without Valerius here anyways.

So he plopped two cubes of sugar into the dark brown fluid and a splash of cream that turned it a golden tan. He stirred it with a spoon that was designed to look like a seashell at the bottom. He then presented the coffee cup to Illarion who glared at it. Caden suppressed a sigh and set it down on top of the table. That gave him a clear view of how his entire plate had been devoured. His stomach rumbled and Iolaire looked mournful.

"So what brings you here to eat your breakfast? Other than showing off that Iolaire's gift finally wore off?" Esme asked tartly.

She gave Caden another look that indicated he should stay and listen. He had been half tempted to leave, but now he saw the wisdom in staying. Illarion would speak far more openly about Iolaire not knowing that Iolaire was right there. So he retreated a few steps to the buffett and stood there as he imagined a proper servant would do. Close enough to spring into action to fill coffee or offer a scone, but far enough away to give the illusion of privacy. He wondered however if he had just watched too many episodes of *Downton Abbey*. Illarion though paid no more attention to him then if he had been no more interesting than the stonework.

Illarion swallowed another bite of buttery croissant before he answered her, "I come to spend time with the Blue Dragon Queen! We have not been in one another's presence in 30-years! It is but a moment, but yet much has happened in that time, yes?"

"We had not seen each other in over a thousand years before that meeting, Illarion, and much has happened in that time too," she answered dryly. "So why are you really here?"

Illarion gave her a wolfish smile. "Ah, Esme, your mousetrap mind is a pleasure!"

"I'm not sure it gives me pleasure to be thought to have a mouse-trap mind." Her voice was as dry as the Sahara now.

Illarion shook a fork at her with a spear of egg upon it. "You are smart. Clever. Very clever. Strategic."

"Yes, well, all of those things are true." Esme inclined her head, perhaps a little flattered in spite of herself. Considering that her intelligence had been a little battered by being betrayed, maybe she needed to hear that.

"Which is why I do not believe you are behind this bombing in the square." Illarion scrapped his teeth over the fork, the yellow eggs disappearing.

Caden's stomach growled again. He surreptitiously grabbed a mini blueberry muffin out of the basket beside him and stuck the whole thing in his mouth after peeling off the paper. He repressed an audible groan as the sweet, rich goodness of the moist muffin smooshed between his tongue and the roof of his mouth.

"Oh, interesting that you think that." Esme shrugged and took another sip of tea. "You came here to give me moral support? Valerius does not believe I'm behind it so that is all that matters."

"Valerius!" Illarion barked and bits of egg covered the table.

Esme's face scrunched up with disgust, but it quickly smoothed back to nonchalance. She handed him her napkin to wipe the wet, partially masticated egg off of his lips and chin. Caden's gorge rose a bit as Illarion negligently smeared the remnants away before tossing the napkin on the table and resuming eating.

"It is Valerius' territory that was affected and he is our..." Esme gestured with her right, beringed hand. The jewels on them flashed in the sunlight as she tried to find the right words.

"He's one of us!" Illarion pounded a fist on the table, which caused the dishes to jump and rattle. "He's not above us! He's not our--"

"King?" She lifted an eyebrow. When he glared at her, face reddening to a tomato-like shade, she continued with an almost sigh, "Illarion, you can shake your fists and cry to the heavens, but Valerius is our leader."

"Only because he has not been challenged!" Illarion spat egg and saliva across the table landing just inches from Esme's lap.

Caden swallowed his muffin and his stomach rumbled again, but not with hunger this time.

"Challenged?" Esme's sculpted eyebrows rose as a smile twitched her lipsticked mouth.

That's total crap! Caden snarled mentally. *You couldn't defeat Raziel if it had both wings tied behind its back!*

Iolaire let out a chirp of agreement.

"I am stronger! Mephous' poison will cause Raziel to drown in its own blood!" Illarion's whole face was suffused with an almost purple color.

"Are you going to challenge Valerius?" Esme held Illarion's gaze steadily.

The passionate response abruptly cooled as Illarion speared another forkful of eggs and grinned at her. "Of course. We will fight over Iolaire."

Caden's cheeks alternately flushed then paled. He was going to be the cause of Valerius and Illarion fighting? Well, that didn't altogether surprise him, but this sounded more serious. Illarion wanted to challenge Valerius. That could lead to war.

Esme let out a trill of laughter. "My dear Illarion, that is the most insane idea you've ever had and that's saying something!"

His green eyes narrowed at her. "Do you think I can't win?"

She shrugged. "In all honesty, no. Not that you won't give it a brilliant go, but in the end, Valerius and Raziel will rip your wings off and use them as floss. But that was not the cause of my laughter."

Caden could see Illarion's jaw working as he clearly was furious that Esme did not think him the winner in this putative battle.

"So what is causing you to laugh at me?" Illarion hissed.

"That you think Iolaire would want you even if you did, in the most unlikely of events, win." Esme held up her teacup to Caden.

He quickly got a warming pot of tea and came over to fill her cup before retreating back to the buffett. He managed to snag a piece of bacon as he set the teapot on the trivet.

"Iolaire must go with the strongest!" Illarion scoffed as he chewed once again with his mouth open.

Esme's eyelids fluttered shut for a moment as if the sight were just too terrible. "I do not believe it works that way."

"Mephous has told me the rules." Illarion leaned back and spread his naked legs. To Caden's horror, his cock stirred as he spoke of Iolaire. "Whoever wishes to mate with Iolaire must challenge and defeat any comers. The last Dragon standing wins."

Caden's mouth fell open with an audible click. He almost spat the bacon onto the floor. He quickly closed his mouth and swallowed it down. He would not waste good bacon on Illarion!

"Scylla tells me otherwise," Esme said after she sipped her tea. "Scylla tells me that while we may challenge each other to prove we are the most worthy of Iolaire, the truth is that Iolaire can choose anyone it wants to mate with."

That's exactly right! Iolaire and I get to choose!

Iolaire twittered softly. But Caden's stomach lurched. He thought of the fact that he wasn't worthy of Iolaire. He had been at the right place at the right time, but Iolaire had been looking for an excuse to join with someone--anyone--in order to be with Raziel. Iolaire and Raziel were destined to be together. Valerius and him... well, if Valerius had any idea of how unworthy Caden was... well, he would be furious and resentful. He wouldn't want to be saddled with Caden.

No, no, I am going to be better. I am going to be worthy of him somehow.

"Bah! Absurd! Even if that is true, Iolaire will choose the strongest! It is only logical," Illarion scoffed as he shoveled in more eggs. "The laws of nature apply to even Spirits."

"And what laws are those?" Esme gazed at Illarion over the top of her cup.

"The strongest make the rules!" Illarion laughed uproariously, clearly in love with his "joke".

Caden rolled his eyes. Esme smothered a look of disgust by sipping her tea at that moment.

"But I am not here to discuss that as I know you are not in the running for Iolaire's hand." Illarion chewed noisily.

Esme winked at Caden. "I don't know, Illarion, I have quite a bit to offer Iolaire."

Illarion's hand with the fork in it froze halfway to his mouth. He stared at her. "Such as what?"

Illarion couldn't quite hide his disbelief. He clearly didn't understand how a mature woman such as Esme could have anything to offer. Caden's eyes narrowed. If he wasn't completely in love with Valerius, she would actually be his second choice. Not for a love match, but for a mentor. Someone he would be willing to support and learn from.

She smiled thinly. "Delights of which you cannot even imagine."

Illarion snorted, but didn't say anything rude, which was the first point in his favor since he had shown up. "I am here to discuss this bombing business."

Esme stiffened. "I can't imagine why."

"It is true that my territory is not convulsed by lawlessness and terror attacks," Illarion said with a shrug. "I rule my people. I do not let them have the illusion that they rule themselves."

"No, I would think that your people have no illusions about such freedom." Esme's smile flattened, but Illarion did not even notice.

"Yes, well, it is best that the people know where they stand. You indulge them and you get chaos." Illarion shrugged again.

"So if your territory is so immune to such chaos since you are so clear with your people, why are you concerned about the bombing?" Esme pressed.

Now that was a good question. Caden grew alert. Was Illarion lying about not having such problems in his territory?   Was this a worldwide conspiracy like Esme had said?

"Do you remember the phrase, 'religion is the sigh of the oppressed creature, the heart of a heartless world, and the soul of soulless conditions. It is the opium of the people?'" Illarion asked. "Or as most people summarize it: religion is the opiate of the masses?"

"Karl Marx. Why?" Esme asked.

"In the beginning, I allowed the Faith into my territory. They worshiped the Spirits and the Dragon Spirits above all, so it seemed harmless. Perhaps even useful," Illarion said as he took a swig of his coffee.

Caden stilled. He had never considered the Faith as a mover in any of the bad things that happened in the world, but now they were seeming more and more suspicious in his eyes. Yet if he thought of the group his mother was a part of, they had always seemed harmless if slightly silly. The dressing in white and singing--God, that song about him and Iolaire!--was so disarming. Could they possibly be behind a worldwide conspiracy to... to do what? Create disasters so that more Spirits emerged into the world?

For one moment that caused him to pause. He had looked up what Iolaire's name was associated with after Wally's reaction to it. It was the name of a yacht that had sunk in 1919 with great loss of life. The yacht had struck rocks just yards from shore and yet 201 out of the 283 people on board had died. It was a disaster. The crowning sorrow of a war. A beautiful yet strange name to choose. Unless it had other meanings.

He looked at Iolaire. The White Dragon Spirit was once again snoozing. Illarion bored it completely. He supposed that it was good that Iolaire was not scared of the Green Dragon. Then again they could will Illarion back to human form at any time they wanted. Well, he hoped that was true. Maybe it had only worked so well because Illarion had not expected him to be able to do that. Maybe now it wouldn't work since he was aware of the possibility or it would be a lot harder to do it.

Esme put her teacup down on its saucer. "Has the Faith done anything in your territory, Illarion?"

"Of course not! I would stamp out any such--such perfidy!"

"And yet, you're bringing it up," Esme pointed out.

Illarion leaned back and shrugged. "There might have been some... small unrest. People claimed that the Spirits wanted to come in, but the Veil had to be pierced."

"Veil had to be pierced?" Esme lowered her head and stared at Illarion hard.

"Do you not know what they believe?" Illarion looked disbelieving.

Caden knew what he was talking about. His mom had babbled often enough about it that he had absorbed most of the Faith's beliefs. One of which was that there was a Veil between this world and the world that the Spirits inhabited. Crises, disasters, tragedies, great acts of heroism or villainy pierced the Veil and allowed the Spirits to come through.

The Faith tracked down as many joinings as they could in order to determine if there were patterns. What they found was that there were more joinings in times of war, starvation, the horrors of slavery, murder and so on and so forth. Tragedies caused clusters of joinings.

But I never thought that the Faith would take that conclusion and try to create more disasters!

"They believe that the Spirits are crying out! They want to find human bodies to inhabit in order to uplift this world!" Illarion let out a bark of laughter. "I suppose it is true, but not in the way that these religious people believe."

"No, I imagine not. Your idea of paradise is not theirs," Esme said tightly.

"Do not act like you want to live in their crazy world!" Illarion waved a hand through the air as if he would topple over a line of crazed cultists.

"No, I do not." She nodded.

"I stamp out one flare of their insanity, only to have it flare in another place and then another and another! No matter what I do--no matter how hard I crack down--they keep coming back!" Illarion slammed his hand against the table again and the cutlery danced.

"The harder you come down on them--the more martyrs you make--you'll only increase the amount of people against you," Esme said sadly. "You cannot use force to end this."

"And what would you have me do? Speak nicely to them? Give them gifts? Accede the demands?" Illarion snorted. "Well, perhaps I will accede to some of them."

"What are their demands?" Esme asked.

Caden wondered that, too. Since the bombing there had been no one claiming credit for it. And that didn't make a lot of sense. Acts of terror were to create, well, terror. Do this or we will kill more! But no one had said anything about what needed to happen to stop the violence.

Illarion gave her a razor-blade smile. "They want a war. A war to end all wars."

HELLFIRE

"Chione, get Mei and bring her to my throne room," Valerius growled. "I did promise her a pyre of her robots."

And that we would roast her upon it! Do not forget that part, Raziel muttered, its red eyes glowing like coals in the dark.

"It will be done," Chione said with a quick nod and she hustled out of the doors to his room, already contacting the security personnel over her tablet to find out exactly where the Red Dragon Queen was.

"Simi, is the robot still in the dungeon?" Valerius asked.

"Yes, it is destroying its brethren," Simi explained.

"What?" That was not what he expected to hear. "Nevermind! Have the Claw retreat! I will deal with this!"

"Yes, my king." Simi crossed one arm over his chest before he was immediately on his com speaking to the Claw.

Valerius did not race past Simi through the doors to get to the dungeon. No, there was a better, faster way. He turned and ran towards the open balcony. He leapt up onto the railing and launched himself into the air, shifting as he tumbled towards the ground. He extended their wings and glided around the curve of the castle to the front where there was an entrance into the dungeon.

People immediately looked up and pointed. Even though seeing him leaving High Reach was a common occurrence, him landing in the courtyard at the lowest level was not. He folded his wings tight to his body just before he shifted back to human form. He took off at a run down the wide stone steps that led to a steel door, six inches thick, that was guarded by half a dozen Claw at the front and over three dozen inside. Although those inside should be evacuating.

I smell burning metal! Raziel growled and pressed close to the front of his chest. The Black Dragon Spirit wanted out again.

As do I. We cannot shift inside the dungeon. Too small. Remember that, Raziel.

The Black Dragon Spirit clawed the ground, but it said, *Then I will give you my strength and my fire.*

Thank you, my friend.

The two Claw in their red and black uniforms did not see him as they were turned towards the door that had held steady against enraged Werewolves, wild Tiger Shifters, even a massive Griffin Shifter whose beak had ripped open plate armor like it was tinfoil. But the door was shuddering now on its massive hinges. The Claw had their weapons drawn and were aiming at the door as stone dust rained down.

"Step back!" Valerius ordered.

The two Claw jumped into the air like frightened kittens. In fact, both of them were Tiger Shifters from what he remembered. This would have amused him if not for the fact that Mei's "gift" was destroying his dungeon.

And her other soldiers, which makes no sense unless their destruction is necessary in order to accomplish her plan.

We will melt them all to slag! Raziel sounded excited.

"Get well behind me," Valerius ordered the Claw.

They dashed behind him just as a large dent appeared in the center of the door. Valerius bared his teeth. There was another crash and the hinges snapped. Valerius gripped the side of the door, his fingers curling around the edges and he pulled.

Shifters were naturally stronger than humans by about a factor of ten depending on the type of Shifter, but to rip a door of this size and weight off its hinges would be near impossible even for the strongest Shifter. But the Dragon Spirits could share strength with their human form and that was what Raziel did for them.

The veins on Valerius' neck bulged as the door groaned then pulled from the threshold like a tooth from a socket. He threw it behind him with a cry. The Claw skittered back farther even though it had not come close to hitting them.

Valerius spun back towards the entry into the dungeon. The dungeon was made up of three one-hundred feet by one-hundred feet rooms interconnected by choke points. The rooms had rows of cells that were made up of a thick nearly indestructible plastic that allowed the guards to see the prisoners from every angle. There was no privacy. And these clear walls allowed Valerius now to see the insane amount of destruction.

The cells were melted, plastic pooling on the floor in superheated lakes. The bunks had been torn from their brackets and were crushed. They looked like strange sculptures. The ceramic toilets were shattered and most were pulverized into dust.

Mei's soldiers lay on the ground in charred and smoking heaps. They were missing limbs. Heads had been twisted off and crushed. Torsos were broken open and the insides snapped and sizzled with electricity. Fluids streamed everywhere. It looked like a battlefield.

No, a slaughter...

But the battle was not over.

There was a seething mass of robots ahead of him at the first chokepoint. Someone had taken a stand there and was still fighting. Bright red laser blasts broke through the mass of soldiers, slagging their middles, and nearly hit Valerius. He dodged out of the way at the last moment. That explained why the door had been failing. The high whine of more lasers going off had Valerius crouching down, but those lasers were aimed towards the choke point.

"What are you doing? STOP!" Mei's voice rose above the whine.

The Red Dragon Queen stood at the base of the stairs. She had on only a short, red silk shift. Her hair was tangled and her face still had the bleariness of sleep imprinted upon it. Mei had clearly been in bed while her robots waged havok. Valerius' eyebrows rose when he caught sight of Chione behind her.

He looked at his Councillor meaningfully. He had ordered her to bring Mei to the throne room, not here. But she had. His temper had his nostrils flaring. But then Chione pointed at the sophisticated looking tablet in Mei's hands. It wasn't exactly a tablet, it was a hologram that was hovering over Mei's right hand while her left one dashed over the hologram.

The robots had all turned towards her for a bare moment, but then a boomerang came out of the choke point and took off more heads and limbs. That had the robots' attention again and they went back to attacking this unseen foe.

Valerius stormed over to the Red Dragon Queen. "Turn them off!"

"I cannot!" Mei cried, her voice tight as her fingers flew over the hologram. "Nothing I do works!"

"Is someone else controlling them?" Chione asked. "Or are they on some kind of self-protection program?"

"Unclear," Mei said through clenched teeth as she furiously tried to control her creations. "They are programmed to protect themselves in a fight, but I have ordered them to not do so."

"And they are not listening. Then they must be stopped in another way," Valerius said.

He knew the hellfire of Raziel rolled through his eyes because Chione gave out a slight gasp. Mei's head jerked up and she realized what was going to happen. Her lips parted.

"Wait--wait--wait! Give me more time!" Mei reached for his shoulder.

Valerius shrugged her off and turned. "There is no more time, Mei. You should never have brought them here."

Valerius allowed the fire to build up inside of him, to fill his veins, his heart, his head, all of him was suffused with hellfire.

Burn them! Raziel roared in excitement.

Valerius opened his mouth and thrust his hands forward. Raziel opened its mouth at the same time. And its hellfire flowed through him. A stream of fire so hot that it was blue white streamed from him and engulfed the backs of the robots nearest to him. They immediately melted, pooling into molten metal around the feet of their fellow soldiers. Robots turned back towards him, realizing that there was an enemy behind them as well as in front. As they turned, he moved his head towards them and the fire followed. He smothered them with fire too.

Laser blasts streaked towards him from the robots on the other side from his flames. They were racing towards him, firing. One blast skimmed his right arm, but there was no searing line of heat. He was fireproof. Other blasts hit his torso and legs. It was like being punched. He staggered back a step but then regained his footing before swinging his head towards his attackers.

Metal flowed like liquid across the stone floor. Fluids turned instantly into steam, shattering the soldiers' torsos and limbs. One managed to race towards him, right arm slagged, left arm raised to strike him. Valerius grabbed it around the throat and breathed fire into its face. It melted away in his hands.

When there were no more laser blasts coming his way and he heard no clank of metal feet on stone did Valerius close his mouth and quench the flames. He looked at the aftermath. The stone floor was mostly obscured by slag, which still smoked and glowed. It was cooling quickly. Most of the cells were completely obliterated or filled with that metal. The whole of this part of the dungeon was destroyed and it would take a long time to restore it. Not that he had many prisoners down here. Thankfully, there had been none at this time or they would have been dead. Only Mei's soldiers had filled this space.

There was a sound from Mei. He looked over at her. She crouched down at the forward edge of the pool of metal and touched it. Her face crumpled and she looked like she would cry for a moment.

"You cry over a bunch of metal?" Valerius hissed. "My Claw could have been killed! My dungeon is a ruin! You will pay for--"

He did not get anything more out as he heard a clank of metal feet coming from the choke point. He had forgotten that the robots had been fighting someone. He had assumed it was Adama, but he had thought that Adama had been slagged with the rest of them. It had not. It emerged from the choke point carrying the head and torso of one of its brethren. Hellfire built in Valerius again.

Chione cried, "Wait! It's not aggressive."

Valerius was about to growl that he didn't care when Adama approached him and knelt on one knee just as it had in the throne room. It offered the head and torso of the other robot as if it was a sacrifice. Valerius scowled.

"For me? Why? You can see that I have made my own trophies. They are melted all over my floor. Perhaps I should do the same to you," Valerius said.

"King Valerius, I have done this to protect you and yours," Adama spoke in that mechanical voice that showed little emotion.

"From what?" Valerius couldn't be that upset about the loss of Mei's soldiers, but the destruction of his dungeon could not be born.

I wish to slag it! Let me slag it! Raziel wheedled, not caring about this "protecting" business. They needed no protection from anyone! Had their demonstration not shown that?

Mei and Chione were suddenly at his side. Mei was glowering at Adama as if she wanted to slag it herself.

"Why did you do this?" She snapped. "Why did you attack your brothers?"

"They are not my brothers. I serve King Valerius and these others serve you," Adama said.

Valerius lifted an eyebrow. He was starting to like this Adama. Maybe a little. Mei blinked and then reared back as if to slap the robot. But she curled her hand into a fist at the last moment and dropped her arm to the side.

"Adama, what do you want Valerius to see in that robot's corpse?" Chione asked.

"May I rise, King Valerius?" Adama asked.

"Yes, you may. Be very careful what you do, Adama. As you can see, my hellfire can destroy you easily," Valerius warned.

The robot rose to its feet then neatly twisted the head from the "dead" robot's body and showed him the inside. There was a cylinder.

Valerius stiffened. Though he did not know what that cylinder was nor how these robots were made, he knew that cylinder had no business there. Mei looked and gave out a gasp.

Echoing his thoughts, she cried out, "That should not be there! I do not know what that is!"

"It is a cylinder containing poison gas," Adama answered. "Certain of these others were fitted with them."

"Oh, by the Gods." Chione brought a hand up to her lips. Her eyes were wide with horror.

The Red Dragon has betrayed us, Raziel growled and smoke and flames flooded out of its mouth.

Valerius slowly turned towards Mei. Hellfire caused his vision to go red. She lifted a hand as she stepped back from him.

"No, Valerius, I did not do this! It would be insane of me to do this!" Mei cried.

"If these robots had released this gas in my city, how many would have died?" Valerius' voice sounded so calm.

"The deaths could have been in the thousands, depending on where they released the gas," Adama answered simply.

His eyes narrowed as rage built. Mei staggered back. For the bandit queen who had never shown fear, she was terrified here. Not even Xipil's scales could save her from his flames.

"How did you know about the gas, Adama?" Chione asked. "Did you see the cylinders being installed?"

"No," Adama answered. "I intercepted a message that was sent to the others to leave here and enter the city to deliver their payload. I had to stop them."

"I did not do this, Valerius!" Mei cried again. "Someone took over control of the soldiers from me!" She held up the hologram she had been tapping on to try and stop the fight. "It wasn't me! Why would I use my own robots to gas your people and be asleep as it was about to happen?"

That caused Valerius to pause. Mei would hardly have been asleep in bed when she knew that he would come after her immediately.

"It does seem unlikely, but you showed bad judgment to bring them here in the first place," Chione said dryly.

"And if it was me why would I give you Adama when it was capable of stopping the attack I supposedly was planning?" Mei kept her eyes on Valerius' face.

That, too, was very true. The fires lowered. Raziel swished its tail angrily though. It wanted to punish Xipil simply for coming here and bringing the tin men in the first place.

"You could have arranged all of this in order for me to trust Adama when you have something else planned," Valerius said, but he didn't believe it. This was all too elaborate, not that Mei was above elaborate plans. Yet unlike her tricking of the mayor and his son long ago, this was too much.

Mei shook her head. She gestured at the carnage. "You have no idea what this has cost me!"

"Money--"

"No, time and materials! These represent years of production! That bastard Illarion will hear of this destruction and he will be encouraged to attack our shared border!" Mei sounded almost shrill and she never sounded shrill.

This was a real concern on her part. The fires died. She wasn't their enemy in this. And she was honestly afraid of Illarion coming after her. Instead of wanting to destroy Mei, he and Raziel almost felt protective of her.

"Mei, considering that your robots were able to be programmed to act against your will perhaps it is best that you not rely upon them in battle?" Chione suggested kindly. "This might have been a good thing in a way."

"No one should have been able to get through my security walls!" Mei slammed one small fist into the palm of her other hand.

"Yet they did," Valerius reminded her and Mei's expression crumpled. She was truly unnerved by this to show so much emotion.

"You intercepted a message, Adama? Can you locate where it came from?" Chione asked the robot.

"It has stopped sending, but I can take you to the last point where the transmission ended," Adama stated.

Mei's head jerked up. "Adama, we must go there! We must find out who did this!" Her small hands fisted at her sides and he saw Mei's temper. "I will kill whoever did this! I will--"

"You will get in line, Mei. I have first dibs," Valerius interrupted her.

"Just leave me something of them," she growled. "Adama--"

"I serve King Valerius only. Do you want me to take you to the location?" Adama asked him.

Valerius was amused by Mei's momentary surprise that again, her creation was not following her orders. She surprised him by laughing at herself.

"I think I programmed him too well." She gave a rueful smile.

"Adama, take us to this place," Valerius ordered.

The mechanical man led them out of the dungeon still carrying the other robot carcass. Valerius took one final glance over his shoulder. He grimaced. Mei was not the only one who had work to restore what was lost today. Adama did not take them very far. In fact, they went only so far as the sculpture garden. The robot pointed to a place right behind a bush cut to look like a Dragon's head roaring at the sky.

"Fitting," Mei remarked sourly. "There appears to be nothing here."

"It would be a little too much to ask that they leave a clue," Chione though sounded downfallen that they hadn't. "Adama, do you see anything we do not?"

The robot though had no further information. "The device they used has been shut off."

"They have given us one clue. They were able to get into High Reach," Valerius growled.

"I'll immediately have the Claw stop anyone from leaving High Reach and go over the footage," Chione said as she brought up her tablet.

"I doubt they are still here or that they left by the main gate or anywhere else there is video coverage," Valerius muttered. "Let us go back to the castle."

As the four of them walked back into the castle's entrance, Mei said, "Are you seeing the pattern of these attacks as I am?"

"What are you seeing?"

"That Serai was associated with Esme and that the soldiers were associated with me," Mei pointed out.

"Someone is trying to cause a war between the Dragons," Valerius suddenly said.

Mei nodded. "Who is behind this? While Illarion is eager for war, he is... well, this is a bit beyond him."

Valerius quirked a smile. "Yes, I tend to agree. Unless he has been hiding his light under a basket this whole time, I think he is out as the mastermind."

They were not able to speak further at that moment as Simi, a phalanx of Claw, followed quickly by Esme, Illarion, Tez and Caden were rushing out of the castle's front doors. Simi and the Claw had known what was happening with the robot war--and Simi looked alarmed at Adama with them--but the others must have sensed his use of hellfire.

"What happened?" Esme cried as she took in Adama carrying a broken robot, Mei in a slip and Valerius naked. Chione looked as put together as always yet it was clear something had happened.

"You used hellfire!" Illarion's eyes were bright with the lust for battle. His head jerked around as he looked for enemies. "I can smell it in the air! But I did not hear Raziel's roar!"

Mei's eyes slid to Valerius. "He used it without shifting."

"Bah, that's impossible!" Illarion waved a hand through the air.

"She is not lying," Esme stated as she stared hard at Valerius. "I did not think it was possible either to use our higher powers when we are not in our Dragon forms, but clearly, I was mistaken."

Valerius said nothing. All of them kept secrets about their powers: what they were, the extent of them, what could and couldn't be used outside of the Dragon form. He had revealed something of himself to them, but he was pleased with the result. Illarion looked stumped.

Tez was suddenly stepping back from him. Esme appeared impressed, but also a little put out. Her use of the Dragon abilities in her human form was legendary. He had never talked about any of his.

At that moment, Caden snaked his way through the crowd to him. Valerius held himself very still. He knew that Caden had revealed himself to Esme, and Mei had seen him in the mirror--though she, too, held herself still--he did not want to reveal Caden's identity to the others if they did not already know. But then Caden threw his arms around Valerius' neck.

"Are you okay? Why did you have to use fire on anybody?" Caden asked.

Valerius wrapped his arms around Caden and ran a hand up and down the boy's back. "I am fine. The robots are not. Adama and I took care of them."

Adama lifted the corpse of the robot it still carried as if it were an exhibit. Caden let out a gasp and looked over at Mei with suspicion. He had texted Valerius the other day about her suspected perfidy.

"Mei is not behind this," Valerius said.

"How can you be so sure?" Esme was now staring at Mei just like Caden was.

"Reasons we will all discuss later," Valerius answered simply.

Illarion gave out an ugly laugh. "So it looks like your mechanical men have a fatal flaw, Mei. Perhaps we should go back to the negotiating table about that land of yours I desire."

Mei stared daggers at Illarion. "Never."

Illarion smirked. "We shall see." He then turned to Caden and Valerius. Frowning, he said, "Dating the help, Valerius?"

Valerius frowned. "The help..."

"He crashed my breakfast with Esme, and ate my bacon." Caden's beautiful face twisted in dismay. "And then assumed I was her servant. So we just went along with it."

"It was quite amusing," Esme said.

"If you are not Esme's servant then who are you?" Illarion demanded.

55

But it was Tez who figured it out. His face alighted with joy. "Iolaire! You are Iolaire!"

He raced forward and grasped both of Caden's hands in his and shook them excitedly.

"Oh, you are exactly what I thought you'd be!" Tez beamed. "Clear eyes. An intelligent brow. A noble nose. A welcoming smile!"

"It's good to meet you too, Tez," Caden assured him, blushing a little at all the compliments.

"What are you talking about, Tez?!" Illarion snapped. He pointed a finger at Caden's chest almost accusingly. "This cannot be Iolaire!"

"Why on Earth not?" Esme asked the enraged Green Dragon Shifter.

"Because!"

"Because?" Chione prompted.

"He is a he and Iolaire is a girl! A woman!" Illarion yelled.

Everyone stared at him. Tez tilted his head to the side as if a different view of Illarion would make sense of that sentence. Caden gazed up at Valerius with a questioning look.

"Why did you assume Iolaire's human counterpart was female?" Esme asked.

"Because Iolaire is--is small and graceful." Illarion looked like he had swallowed lemons.

"That is so stupid," Tez said with a shake of his head. "But what does it matter that Caden is male? I don't--"

"Illarion does not like men romantically. He has, in fact, made many homophobic remarks to his people in his addresses yet he has also proclaimed Iolaire his mate. What will you do now, Illarion? Eat your words?" Valerius remarked with a grin on his lips. "And it seems that you really did have some romantic interest then, didn't you, Illarion, in Iolaire? Well, well, it seems one learns something new everyday."

Illarion continued to open and shut his mouth as he gestured at Caden as if it simply could not be and that his disbelief would change Caden into the shapely woman he'd likely been imagining. Everyone else just shook their heads and proceeded to ignore the Green Dragon Shifter.

"Adama, go with Captain Simi and take the robot with you to be examined," Valerius ordered.

"Valerius, let me assist in this," Mei suggested. "I know more about them than anyone."

Valerius nodded after a moment. "Queen Kaila will be here in a few hours. I suggest we hold off on any discussions until then." He looked down at Caden. "I need to feed you bacon in the meantime since Illarion so cruelly stole yours."

GREATER POWER

"Before bacon," Caden began as he turned to look up at Valerius' handsome face, "I want to see what you destroyed!"

Valerius' full lips quirked into a smile. "Something you want *before* bacon? Now that is a surprise."

Caden's mouth opened and shut. "Okay, I'd like both at the same time, but if I must choose, I guess hellfire and destruction first."

Chione had stopped her instructions to the Claw to review the videos of who had triggered Mei's robots to go on a rampage. "Do not worry, Caden. I will have bacon sent to you."

"Really?! How fancy! You don't have to do that!" Caden laughed self-consciously.

He really should get his own bacon. Chione had more important things to do, but she was already talking to someone in the kitchen so it was a done deal.

"Not at all! I know Valerius will enjoy showing you his handi-work," Chione said.

Iolaire's tongue lolled out at the thought of bacon. Caden's stomach rumbled. He'd hardly had a chance to eat before Illarion had spoiled things. At that moment, a Claw appeared with a red silk robe for Valerius. The Black Dragon King shrugged it negligently on. Caden immediately mourned the loss of that beautiful form. Valerius didn't seem to notice Caden's discrete ogling, but said instead, "You must be curious about this then to give up bacon immediately!"

"It is worth seeing," Mei remarked. "As you will find out... I want to call you Iolaire but--"

"Caden. My name is Caden," he corrected her gently.

She nodded. "Caden. As you will find, being able to use your Dragon gifts in your human form is rare. Being able to use one's greater Dragon powers in your human form is unheard of."

"Until now," Esme said with a lifted eyebrow at Valerius.

"Hellfire--it is called hellfire, right?--is a greater power?" Caden asked Valerius.

"Hellfire is impressive," Valerius answered, but it wasn't really an answer.

More raised eyebrows from Esme. "Are you suggesting, Valerius, that hellfire is not one of your greater powers? That it is just ordinary?"

Valerius smirked. "I must have some secrets, Esme."

"If I ever considered you an open book I will now eat those words," Esme laughed not unkindly.

"So! Show me this destruction?" Caden pressed, bobbing up and down on his heels.

"Of course." Valerius looked a little pleased.

Iolaire was wide-eyed in Caden's chest, clearly excited and a little nervous to see evidence of just how powerful Valerius and Raziel were.

"I look forward to speaking to you later, Caden, Valerius. I will tell you what I find about my robots." Mei then swept out of the room following a clanking Adama and a straight-backed Captain Simi.

"You cannot leave us now, Caden!" Tez's lower lip wibbled. "We have just found you! And look at Illarion's face! He is so desperate to be around you as well!"

That had a smile appearing on Tez's own mouth for just a moment. Illarion, however, did not smile. In fact, his eyes narrowed and his expression darkened. He turned on his heel and stalked off, not saying a word.

"I guess he doesn't want to be mates with me anymore," Caden remarked dryly.

"What a shame," Valerius' tone was even drier.

Caden grinned up at him. "And here I was worried about revealing who I was to everybody. This is going great!"

Valerius embraced him and kissed the top of his head. When they broke apart--though Valerius kept one hand firmly on Caden's lower back--Caden looked over at Tez and Esme. Tez's hands were clasped in front of his chest and he was beaming at them with suspiciously moist eyes. Esme was smiling like a proud grandmother. Caden pinked.

"Ah, do you guys want to see the destruction, too?" Caden asked them.

To his surprise and delight, both of them nodded eagerly. Valerius led the four of them out of the castle and into the courtyard towards a set of broad, wide steps around the corner. Caden and Valerius held hands while Tez gentlemanly offered his arm to Esme. As they walked, Tez peppered Caden with questions and statements.

"You are so young!" Tez remarked. When Caden smiled uncertainly, Tez continued, "It is not a criticism. I mean how can one be criticized for one's age? It is chosen for us and our concept of time continues it for us. It's a conceit really. But what I meant is that I am so used to Shifters looking young, but not really *being* young. Do you understand? And for a Dragon Shifter to be so--so--"

"Innocent?" Valerius' lips twitched.

"No! Fresh! That is the word I was looking for," Tez said with a "bah" at Valerius.

"Innocent. Inexperienced. Very new. Fresh, I guess works, too," Caden admitted.

"You're bold to be so open with us, Caden. Most Shifters try to be cagey," Esme remarked, but she was smiling gently at him. It wasn't a criticism, or maybe it wasn't a criticism about talking to them this way, but maybe not to others.

"I think if I were to describe myself as anything else, it would be hard to believe anything I said," Caden explained.

"So not only is being a Shifter--a Dragon Shifter, no less--new to you, but the world is!" Tez looked rather stunned at the thought of it. He shook himself. "It is good that we are all here then."

"Good?" Valerius had that dry tone again. "I thought you were here to woo him, Tez?"

Tez smiled at Valerius and waved a hand as if any such thought was foolish. "I was here to meet him above all. But now, I see that we must all work together to help him. To teach him. It is so exciting! I have always wished to have another Dragon to train!"

"Caden isn't a pet, Tez," Esme reminded him gently.

"Y-yes, I know." Tez's quick glance at Caden told Caden that he was thinking of him a little bit as a pet.

"Though Iolaire is adorable," Esme added.

"Yes!" Tez was jubilant again.

"But not as pretty as Eldoron?" Valerius was actively suppressing a smile as he said this.

Tez shrugged. "No other Dragon is."

"Eldoron is beautiful," Caden said kindly.

"Oh, Eldoron is so pleased! Eldoron thinks that Iolaire and it should fly together. Gold and white! Such a pair! The people of Reach would have never seen such beauty." Tez stretched a hand out to the sky as if he could imagine it right then and there.

"Uhm, that would be great, but you did see how hard it was for me to land last night, right? I'm still learning," Caden reminded him. "Valerius makes sure that I don't squash anybody or anything."

Valerius tightened his hand around Caden's. "And Valerius would be a part of any flying."

Caden grinned up at him. He really only wanted to fly with Valerius anyways.

"Talking about yourself in the third person now, Valerius?" Esme teased.

"If I must to get my point across." Valerius rubbed a thumb along the back of their linked hands.

"I don't know if black goes so well with white and gold," Tez sighed. "But if it must be, it must be."

"It must," Valerius said simply.

They'd reached the top of an impressive set of stone steps that curved downwards into the side of High Reach. There were torch holders on either side of the stairs. Caden thought that if there were lit torches it would look quite like the entrance to a medieval dungeon. But the thick metal door that lay sprawled below them, like a fallen soldier, the illusion was broken. Caden released Valerius' hand and clattered down the steps. He knelt down and touched the metal. The hinges were wrenched off. He couldn't imagine the force it took to cause the door to be like this.

"The robots did this?" Caden looked up at Valerius.

The Black Dragon King's hands were slid into the robe's pockets. He moved with his usual predatory grace. A faint smile was on his lips that was almost embarrassed.

"No, I did," Valerius answered, stopping a step above him.

"Seriously?" Caden's voice was hardly above a whisper as he looked back down at the door that likely weighed half a ton.

"Dragon Shifters are very strong," Tez told him helpfully.

"I know, but..." Caden shook his head as he slowly got to his feet. "I just didn't think... I don't know. I guess seeing is believing."

"And doing is even better," Esme said. "Why don't you try to lift it, dear?"

Caden's eyes widened and he wiped his hands on his jeans. "Oh, I couldn't do that! I--"

"You are a Dragon Shifter! Of course, you can!" Tez enthused.

Caden's gaze slid to Valerius. Surely, the Black Dragon King would put an end to this silliness! He was a Dragon Shifter sure! But he was a little Dragon Shifter. And he wasn't in his Dragon form now!

"Go ahead. Lift it," Valerius said with a tip of his head. When Caden gave him a "you're crazy look" he added, "One-handed."

"What?!" Caden squawked. "You're making this even more impossible!"

Valerius just smiled. "You can do this, Caden."

Caden muttered, "Don't laugh if I can't do this. I might manage to nudge it maybe. Maybe."

Iolaire twittered at him, blinking, and shuffling its wings happily. Caden didn't know if Iolaire thought he could do this or was simply giving encouragement. Caden leaned over and put the fingers of his right hand underneath the door. He fully expected to have to strain to even make it wobble. So he put his all into it and the door flew upwards and then fell down again on the other side before sliding down a few more steps. Caden's mouth opened in a gasp. Iolaire let out a triumphant coo.

"WHOA! Did you see that?" Caden whipped around to face Valerius.

The Black Dragon King was smiling. "I did."

He looked at Esme and Tez. "You saw that, too, right? That was so cool!"

Both Dragon Shifters smiled encouragingly at him. Tez clapped.

"So fresh, you see! Everything is new again!" Tez stated. "It makes me feel like anything is possible once more! It makes me remember the gift that being a Shifter is."

Caden caught sight of Valerius' face out of the corner of his eye. There was a sudden understanding expression on the Black Dragon King's face. He felt the same as Tez, and Caden was pretty sure that he felt some of Tez's excitement at Caden experiencing this whole new world. There was a clattering sound as the door shifted and slid down a few more steps, all but blocking their path.

"Uhm…" Caden began. "Should I try to move that?"

"You've had enough fun with that door for today. Let me." Valerius leaned over and with one hand lifted the door up and handed it to Esme. "Would you put that up above us, Esme?"

"Of course," Esme answered.

She took the door with the same ease and lightly tossed it back up onto the courtyard. It landed with a clatter. Caden couldn't help the gasp of awe he let out.

"Okay, I'm sorry, but that was so incredibly cool!" Caden laughed.

Esme curtseyed and let out a delighted, young girl's giggle. The four of them shared a look then. There was a connection here. For the first time, Caden didn't feel completely singular. The connection he had begun to have with Valerius grew even as he felt new connections--not as strong, but still there--with Esme and Tez.

"I'm really glad to have met you," Caden suddenly said.

"Yes, dear, I am too," Esme told him as she nodded.

"Most certainly! If, for nothing else, to see Illarion so humiliated!" Tez slapped his thigh with childish glee.

"I second that," Valerius murmured even as he caressed Caden's cheek with the back of one hand.

Caden's gaze slid to the other two Dragon Shifters to see what they thought of this open display of affection. He had started it by running to Valerius and revealing himself, not caring about his secret or anything else, but after smelling that bitter, metal fire and feeling the earth tremble... he'd have done anything to make sure Valerius was okay. A knowing, fond look was on Esme's face. Tez just seemed fascinated as if he were watching a bear playing the ukulele.

"So are we going to see the results of hellfire?" Caden asked even as his cheeks burned.

After witnessing what was possible with the door, Caden really wanted to see the destruction. Valerius linked their nearest hands together and led them down the stairs.

"Esme, I thought only you could use magic when you weren't in Dragon form," Caden said over his shoulder.

"Magic?" Esme let out a laugh. "Oh, well, I suppose our powers are that. But no, every Dragon can use some of their powers in human form."

"But which ones and how many are kept secret from everyone!" Tez explained.

"Oh? But why--oh, my God," Caden breathed the last as they stepped through the doorway and entered the dungeon.

The floor was covered in gleaming metal. It was no longer liquid anymore, but a solid two-inch thick layer over three-quarters of the stone floor. There were unrecognizable chunks of parts of the robots that hadn't completely turned to slag.

"All those robots... oh, man, Mei must be pissed," Caden laughed softly.

"More upset that someone got past her precious firewall protecting her control of them," Valerius answered.

Tez whistled as he and Esme spread out to survey the wreckage.

"You are formidable, Valerius," Tez remarked approvingly. "I mean I knew that, but still... seeing is believing. I am like Caden in my shock and admiration."

"Illarion should see this." Esme was tapping her chin and looking over the carnage with an almost cold approval.

"Why?" Caden asked.

"You heard him, Caden. He thinks he could win in a battle between Valerius and himself. This would show him how foolish such a belief is," she answered.

Caden felt as much as saw Valerius tense and his eyes narrow. His temper and the violence that he controlled so well were suddenly right beneath the surface. A tissue-thin layer of civilization was hiding the Black Dragon King beneath. Caden's breath caught and he looked at Valerius. The moment Valerius saw the fear in his face, the violence bled out of him and he cupped Caden's cheek.

"I won't let Illarion even try to attack you. I'll make it so he can never shift again!" Caden's hands fisted at his sides.

Iolaire let out a trill of agreement.

"So fierce." Valerius smiled at him fondly. "But I think that a confrontation between Illarion and myself is inevitable. Illarion must put his hand in the fire and be burned before he realizes he can be harmed."

"You shouldn't do that!" Caden cried.

"What? Why?" Valerius looked between them.

Esme sighed and tilted her head towards Tez. "Caden."

"I know I suck at secrets!" Caden cried. "But I know we can share this with Tez. I feel it. Iolaire feels it."

"Tell Tez what?" Now Tez was speaking in the third person.

Iolaire was cocking its head as it cooed--not in the same way as it did at Raziel--at Tez. Tez's eyes grew huge and he put a hand on the center of his chest.

"Iolaire! I can--I can see it! It is cooing at me and Eldoron!" Tez now was weeping with joy. "Oh, Eldoron and I are now complete!"

Valerius looked at Caden. "Iolaire is... is cooing at them?"

Caden grinned and put a hand on Valerius' arm. "Not the way Iolaire does to you and Raziel."

And then Caden blushed so hard that his cheeks felt they were on fire. He might have just revealed more than he should. Despite him having seen how the separation between Iolaire and Raziel was breaking down, he didn't think Valerius knew. He wasn't sure why. Maybe it was because Valerius was too close to see it, that things had been the same for so very long.

"I see." It was Valerius' turn to blush. He lowered his head and wouldn't quite meet Esme and Tez's eyes.

"Esme, tell them about the Faith and war," Caden urged her.

With a deep breath, Esme nodded and pressed the tips of her fingers together beneath her chin before telling Tez and Valerius everything they had learned from Illarion and her own investigation into Serai.

Caden turned to Tez. "Have there been any violent activities by the Faith in your territory, Tez?"

Tez's forehead furrowed, but then shook his head. "The Faith is not strong in my territory. You see, my territory is filled with many native peoples who were forced to accept Christianity. What they did was to incorporate their already existing beliefs and Christianity. When Shifters were revealed to be real, they just... well, incorporated some more. Christianity just got a larger pantheon, but nothing truly changed."

Esme crossed her arms over her chest. "I suppose you were lucky in a way, Tez. Belief in religion in my territory was all but gone. It still remained in a sort of historical almost secular way, but after Shifters were revealed to be real... It was like a tidal wave drowned everyone in shock. Their minds--so used to believing there was nothing more than what they could experience with their five senses--suddenly were shown to be completely unreliable. The Faith has taken off there. Sometimes... sometimes it worries me."

"Even though you have used it to control your territory at times?" Tez pointed out.

Esme waved a hand through the air. "I know that you think of yourself as a Dragon of the people, Tez, but you must understand that I am not you and my people are not yours."

Tez bowed to her. "You are right. Forgive me, Esme. I just remember how the powerful ruled the peasants through religion in the past. It... grates."

"Of course, it does! You were controlled in the past. Not the controller. Now you seek to give people choice and the illusion, if nothing else, that they are in control of their destiny," Esme said. "But if the Faith truly is seeking to sow discord among us then not even your territory with your faithful little workers will not be safe for long."

"We can't have a war! That would be crazy! So many people would die!" Caden looked at what Valerius had done with hellfire. "So many people would die."

Valerius grasped his chin and forced Caden to look at him. "Do not be afraid, Caden."

Caden caught hold of Valerius' wrist. "How can I not be? They're going to use me and Iolaire as proof that their crazy plan is the right one! Plant a bomb and get the ninth Dragon Shifter! What are a few lives compared to that?"

Caden's words caused a hush to fall over all of them. He knew he was right. Iolaire was making low, sad sounds. It, too, feared that violence was coming, a tidal wave of it, and that it would touch all of them, and more.

"How do we stop this?" Tez lifted his hands into the air in helplessness.

"How do we stop what?" A bright voice came from the doorway.

All of them turned to see a golden-skinned woman who stood over six-feet. Her arms and midriff were bare. She wore a top of what looked like folded green banana leaves and a multi-layered skirt that came to her knees. Her feet were bare and she held what looked like a hoverboard in her right hand. Long black hair that hung in loose waves down to her waist framed an expressive, pretty face.

"Kaila!" Esme proclaimed and immediately enfolded the newcomer in an embrace.

"Esme, my dear sister! My fellow water goddess, how I have missed you!" Kaila proclaimed.

They bussed each other's cheeks before breaking off and looking at one another with evident fondness. Kaila caught sight of Caden over Esme's shoulders and her bright blue eyes fixed on Caden. She walked slowly towards him, a look of almost awe on her handsome features. She lightly took his hands in hers.

"Ninth Dragon Shifter," she murmured. "I am Kaila, the Turquoise Dragon, and Queen of the Seas."

NEVER BE BORING

"Come on, Valerius, get on my hoverboard!" Kaila leaned down and wiggled her fingers at him as she said it. As if he was a wild animal she wanted to lure to its doom.

"No," Valerius said with a shake of his head as he leaned back in his chair.

They were out in the courtyard. Chione had promised to bring Caden bacon in the dungeon, but one whiff of the fire and brimstone in the dungeon had her backing out, waving a hand in front of her face, and telling them she would have a table set out in the *fresh* open air.

That was where he, Caden, Esme, Tez and Kaila now were. The table was laden with so much food that it was practically groaning. But the way Caden was inhaling the food--especially the bacon, he'd growled when Tez had even *looked* at the platter--there very well might not be enough. Valerius found himself smiling fondly at the young man. He knew it was ridiculous for him to find a normal Dragon Shifter's appetite endearing. The way Esme smirked at him told him that *yes*, it was ridiculous, but she found *him* endearing none-theless too.

"Pretty please?" Kaila was now threatening to pout, but unlike Caden's puppy eyes, he was unmoved.

"No," he repeated.

She wishes us to fall on our butt and then laugh at us, Raziel snorted and placed its massive head on its forearms.

Indeed, Valerius remarked dryly.

She always laughs at us. More snorts from Raziel.

I think that is one of her powers. To make one feel ridiculous. How can one pretend to be a big, strong Dragon on one's butt? Valerius muttered.

Kaila was standing while the rest of them were seated. She had the hoverboard on the ground with her bare left foot on it. She was moving it back and forth. It glided smoothly about six inches off the stones. It seemed solid and easy to use, but it would *not* be.

Kaila sighed. "I realize that you have never *surfed*, Valerius, so your balance might not be what mine is." She splayed a hand across her chest. He knew that she was trying to goad him into trying the hoverboard. "But I'm sure you're not so *clumsy* as to be unable to simply stand on my board."

"You sound so reasonable, Kaila," Esme said, but her lips were twitching suspiciously.

"I am." Kaila's head tipped back. She was looking at the skies as if the heavens themselves proclaimed how reasonable she was, and how unreasonable he was.

"I am still not getting on that hoverboard," Valerius murmured as he popped a grape into his mouth.

Her head snapped towards him and her sparkling eyes narrowed. If she did not look so cute, the effect would have been greater.

Not against us. Raziel stretched out a claw and spread its toes.

"Fine! Be uncool! Be *boring!*" Kaila's hands were on her hips. "Be an old, fuddy duddy!"

"I think she knows you too well, Valerius," Tez chuckled as he tucked into a cheese and ham omelet.

It was Valerius' turn to narrow his eyes. "So if I am an old fuddy duddy, what are you, Tez? Why aren't you jumping on that infernal device to ride it around and show us *olds* how its done?"

Caden made a choking noise, which had Valerius thumping his back. Red-faced, Caden thanked him and then said, "Olds? You almost sounded--"

"Hip?" Esme chuckled.

Valerius just shrugged and turned back to Tez. "I am waiting for you to get on that hoverboard."

Tez looked alarmed. He had that deer in the headlights look. Eldoron was very particular about always looking its best. Tez falling on his ass would not fit in with that look.

What lie will he make up? Raziel's claws clacked as it put one toe down at a time.

"I'm eating right now." Tez's cheeks were burning as he stuffed so much omelet into his mouth that he couldn't even speak.

Kaila let out a moan and stomped her foot on the hoverboard which bobbled and nearly slid out from under her. She quickly caught her balance though and pretended it hadn't happened.

"Caden, surely *you* want to try my hoverboard?" Kaila's lower lip thrust out at him.

Caden--still chewing bacon, Chione was on a phone call with the president so he might have to ask for more bacon himself--looked at the hoverboard, at Kaila's pleading face, then over at Valerius' neutral expression before looking back at the hoverboard.

"I heard that they banned hoverboards because they're dangerous," Caden finally said.

"Caden! Oh, you mustn't be afraid! I'll make sure you're safe! We have a connection already and I would never let anything happen to you!" Kaila's eyes were simply *shining*.

"You really can't get hurt, Caden dear. Remember that we're Dragon Shifters. Practically indestructible. Remember how you lifted that door? Same thing here but with invulnerability," Esme reminded him. "That's not why these two chickens--I mean brave Dragon Shifters--won't try it."

"Why won't they?" Caden's eyes were wide with curiosity.

"Dignity. They are afraid of their dignity being bruised," she said.

"Yes! Yes!" Kaila bounced up and down on the hoverboard, managing to keep her feet rather remarkably.

"I don't understand. You guys are all... well, not graceful, but very athletic!" Caden cried loyally.

Kaila leaned towards Caden and curled one hand around her mouth as she whispered, "Raziel has a *big butt* and therefore tends to tip back. Now you may say that doesn't matter because it is Valerius using the hoverboard, but I tell you that it translates. Big dragon butts have an impact on the human form."

Caden stared at her silently for a long moment, but then he was laughing so hard that he was pounding the table. "Oh, God, I can see that! I can so--Valerius, don't be mad! I love Raziel's butt! Iolaire loves Raziel's butt!"

Valerius was scowling at him. Raziel's head had lifted from its forearms to also scowl at Caden. Caden swallowed.

Tez murmured, "I would imagine Caden enjoys Valerius' butt very much for many reasons."

Kaila held up a hand and showed it tipping backwards. "Tip. Right on the ass!"

Then everyone was laughing, even Valerius. Raziel just shook its massive head and laid it down. Its big butt was a powerful butt and it would make sure that Kaila's Spirit Lana remembered that the next time they flew together. That had Valerius' smile growing.

"What part of Eldoron is causing Tez to be... ah, ungainly on the hoverboard?" Caden asked as he wiped his tears from his eyes.

Tez straightened. "Nothing! Eldoron is perfect!"

Kaila's eyes were narrowed as she studied Tez critically as if she could see through him to Eldoron. "I think the biggest part of Eldoron is..."

Tez looked like he was awaiting a pronouncement of doom.

"... is..."

Tez quivered.

Then she smiled and said, "It's heart! A big heart."

"Yes! Exactly." Tez went back to happily buttering toast.

"What about you, Esme? Are you going to take a ride on the hover-board?" Caden asked the Blue Dragon Shifter.

"Oh, not with these shoes, dear." She gracefully extended one foot and showed an expensive high heeled shoe.

"But you can take them off, Esme!" Kaila waggled her bare left foot.

"No, darling. The shoes go with the outfit. Remove them and it doesn't work," Esme said as she took a bite of a scone followed by a sip of tea.

Caden smirked and went back to his bacon even as Kaila looked utterly crestfallen. She wouldn't get any victims today for her hoverboard.

"Perhaps Illarion will try your hoverboard, Kaila," Tez said with a titter.

Kaila's eyes widened with alarm as she flipped the hoverboard up into her arms and clutched it to her chest. "I wouldn't let him touch Dolly!"

"Dolly?" Caden asked.

Kaila stroked the hoverboard, which Valerius noted had the image of a dolphin on it.

"My favorite dolphin. She's amazing. Truly amazing. I couldn't bring her here, obviously, because there is no ocean." Her lips writhed back from her teeth as if it was quite distressing. "So I painted her on my hoverboard and now she's with me even here in this practical desert."

Valerius felt piqued. "It is *not* a desert. This is a temperate zone."

"Desert," Kaila murmured under her breath.

"Well, I doubt that Illarion will make an appearance anytime soon," Esme said with a soft huff of laughter. "He's recovering from the reality of Caden and Iolaire."

"What reality?" Kaila looked interested again.

Caden let out a groan and let his head tip back.

"He thought Caden was a girl!" Tez snickered.

"Okay." Kaila looked as bewildered as Tez had at first, too. "And?"

"He's not," Esme said as she looked very amused.

"I don't follow." Kaila's brow scrunched.

"He said we were mates, but is only into women sexually, I guess. It's a terrible, horrible story and I'm just glad that it's over before it began," Caden told her quickly. He then narrowed his eyes at her. "You knew I was the White Dragon Shifter immediately."

"Of course! Which is why this is all so confusing about Illarion..." Kaila's brow was still scrunched.

"How did you know that, dear?" Esme asked as she wiped her hands on her napkin.

"It's my sight!" Kaila answered brightly.

No one looked brightly back in return. Everyone looked flummoxed in all honesty.

"If a person is in their Spirit form, I can see their human form and vice versa!" Kaila explained.

"Oh, that's cool! So I couldn't have ever kept my identity secret from you..." Caden looked disturbed.

Valerius was and wasn't surprised. It explained some things such as how Kaila always seemed to anticipate attacks from other Shifters. Basically, she would be able to anticipate the types of powers to be used against her. He wondered how far her sight went.

"Yes, it's fun!" Kaila beamed. "So... what are we going to do? Huh? Huh?"

"Uhm, eat and then... I was hoping to nap," Caden admitted with a shy look at Valerius.

"Nap?" She exaggerated her lip movements as she repeated Caden's word. "You can't be serious? It's a beautiful day!"

"Yeah, napping in the sun is awesome." Caden's head tilted to the side and his eyes glazed over as he talked of naps. "You like naps in the sun, too, right, Valerius?"

"I do," Valerius said.

"Big butt," Kaila whispered.

He shot her a look that had her grinning. "But we have to do something fun! We're all here and we're *never* together. We can't just waste the time!"

"You do have a point, Kaila," Esme said.

"Yes! Maybe we can do a fake aerial battle!" Kaila started to describe the scene. "Valerius can chase Caden past each of us. We do our powerful attacks--just missing him of course--but to the people below it will look real! There will be dive bombing of the crowds. People will shout and clap and--"

"Scream?" Tez raised an eyebrow.

"Not if we tell them we're just doing a show! Like the most ultimate show on Earth!" Kaila enthused. "Just look at how excited people were to watch Iolaire and Raziel fight!"

"That wasn't good. People died, Kaila. It wasn't for fun." Caden shivered and Valerius held him tighter.

"Oh, yes, of course, you're right. That--that was terrible, but I was just thinking about how much my people love to see me use my powers while the rest of you hide yours ever so much."

"Maybe a fake battle later? When people are less edgy after all the bombs and stuff," Caden suggested.

"Indeed, speaking of the bombs," Esme began.

Esme folded her napkin and placed it beside her plate. She looked meaningfully at Valerius to see if he wanted to bring Kaila into the know about the possible war on the world by the Faith. Valerius had no doubts about Kaila. She had nothing to do with any of this. Her butterfly-like mind was immune to such zealotry. And though like all of them, Kaila could be fierce, she did not have the desire to hold onto anything--especially anger and hatred--for long. So Valerius nodded.

"We were all discussing the bombings and current events," Esme began.

"Oh, boring! Gah! Esme, don't let us talk about those terrible things!" Kaila stuck out her tongue. "I didn't think of them at all which is why I didn't realize the fake attack wouldn't be good!"

"But it's important, Kaila," Caden said earnestly.

"Yes, yes, I know! But..." Kaila struggled to find the words for what she felt, but finally she found them and they rushed out in a torrent, "There has always been hatred in people's hearts and there always will be. It's pointless to think you can change that. And pointless things are boring!"

"If it was just trying to stop people from hating, I would agree with you," Caden said carefully. His earnest heart could not imagine clearly not trying to fix things. "But this is a conspiracy to cause death and chaos. We can stop that."

"Perhaps!" She set the hoverboard down and started to glide around the table in a large circle. "But violence is inevitable. Death and chaos are inevitable."

"Why do you say that?" Tez blinked at her.

"Because there's an imbalance." Kaila though was perfectly balanced as she spun around.

"Between humans and Shifters?" Caden asked.

"Yes. And between humans and humans. And between Shifters and Shifters," Kaila explained as she stretched her arms upwards, fluttering her fingers in the sunlight. "But yes, the most obvious overall imbalance is between humans and Shifters. Humans thought they were on top for a very long time. Now, they see they are not. And those that are wise enough to see that know things are not going to get better for humanity in the years ahead."

Valerius frowned. "I do not see why we cannot sustain some kind of balance through--"

"Our influence? Our wills?" Kaila stopped gliding and stared at him as if he had suddenly turned into a frog. "Valerius, you, of all people, I thought would understand this! You've kept your hands off things in the past but now you want to try and mold the world?" Then her eyes flickered between him and Caden. She noted the arm he had around Caden's shoulders. The way Caden snuggled against him. A sad smile crossed her face. "Ah, I see!"

"What do you see?" Valerius growled. If she was going to think that his desire to stop the current violence that was ongoing was some kind of lovesick action, he would have words with her.

Raziel, however, did not seem to think this was a problem. It murmured, *Iolaire is worth much. I would have this world sing for Iolaire.*

Yes, as I would for Caden. But she intimates that we are being blind to reality because of our... affections, Valerius pointed out to his Spirit. *I feel much more clear-sighted than I have ever been! Like I have woken after a*

76

deep sleep and now am fully awake once more! Do you not feel this way, Raziel?

I do, but that it comes from love does not make it any less. Raziel closed its eyelids as it said this.

Love...

Raziel started to snore.

Are you in love with Iolaire? Valerius asked the sleeping Spirit. *Did you just tell me that Iolaire is your mate and then start snoring?*

Raziel continued to snore.

"You want to make the world a better place for Caden." Kaila's sad smile remained. He was about to shout at her that this wasn't the case when she added, "That's very commendable. I wish my heart was so full that I wanted to try and change the world... well, you get my point."

"We guide the world, Kaila. I think we're quite capable of moving things, if just a little," Esme said almost coldly.

She had reason to believe she could guide things. She'd guided many kingdoms for a long time. She'd made *history* what it was some would say.

"Oh, Esme, dearest, I didn't mean to say that we--or maybe *you*-- couldn't change this, but some things are inevitable no matter how much we nibble around the edges!" Kaila hovered over behind the Blue Dragon Shifter and put her hands on Esme's shoulders. "Because, in the end, controlling this is like trying to control the ocean itself. You can make waves here and smooth seas there, but in the end... the water flows as it will."

Valerius understood her position. In his most dour, people-doubting moments, he and Raziel wanted to just fly up to the tallest mountain peaks and never come down. People were awful. People were often monstrous. People often deserved to die. But, then again, there were so many who were wonderful and angelic and deserved a life worth living. Maybe he did view things differently with Caden here. Maybe she wasn't altogether wrong about that.

"Caden has had an effect on me," Valerius finally said. He reached up and drew his fingers through Caden's curls. Caden immediately turned and smiled at him. "He's made me realize that we need to not have a world where nihilism reigns. I do want a world that he will love and continue to love."

Caden kissed his cheek. "Just knowing you want to try is huge."

Valerius kissed his temple. Tez's chin was resting in his hands as he gazed at them.

"You make me believe in true love again," Tez sighed. "To think that we all came here to court Caden!"

"Speak for yourself. I came for friendship." Esme put a hand on her chest. "I knew Valerius would never let Iolaire go when it appeared in his territory first."

Caden stared at her. "You really thought that?"

"Oh yes, from the moment he complained about you, I knew what the end result would be," Esme said.

"So then I don't have to worry about you all courting me? I mean, it's clear that Illarion is out," Caden said.

"Oh, but courting you would be fun!" Kaila protested. Before Valerius could growl anything, she added, "But I like girls like Illarion likes girls so it would be like courting you as a *friend*. A very good friend."

Caden frowned, but then his expression cleared. "You have my friendship, Kaila. But I would like to get to know you one on one. I'd like to get to know all of you that way. And together."

"Yes, we must do that." Tez rubbed his hands together as if he couldn't wait to get started.

A faint alarm bloomed in Valerius' chest, but he immediately squashed it. Because he knew that Caden wanted to be with him. And the young Shifter should take advantage of befriending the other Dragon Shifters while they were here. Now. Because he wasn't going to let Caden go to any other territory any time soon. And he would never let Caden go by himself.

"So I would like to have some time with you now, Caden. Can we do something now?" Kaila pleaded.

At that moment, there was a buzz and Caden fumbled in his

pockets to get his phone. "Sorry, guys, but this is a special phone so I need to answer. It has to be important."

Valerius leaned towards Caden as he brought out the phone, wondering what disaster had befallen his territory now. He saw that it was Rose calling. He thought of Rose as a moderating influence on Caden's innocence. She had been through the hard knocks of life. She knew the world could be cruel. So he wasn't worried just by seeing her name on the screen.

Caden answered the phone, "Hey, Rose, what's up?"

When he saw all of the Dragon Shifters staring at him, he shifted a little. Then Esme turned her head, pretending not to listen, as she studied the city down below. Tez found the remnants of his omelet fascinating. Kaila was already genuinely bored and looking for something to do.

Valerius' hearing though was locked on Rose's tone, which was *higher* than usual, "Hey, Caden, uhm... slight problem."

"What? What's wrong? Something up at Wally's?" Caden lowered his voice as he asked, "Did he get buried in an avalanche of plushies again?"

"What?" Rose laughed. "No, no, Wally's *fine*. But... uhm, I did something stupid."

Caden sat up straight. "Are you okay? Do you need help?"

Rose let out a sigh. "You're always so--so..." She sighed again. "I may have mentioned to Marban your idea about bringing Iolaire to the Below."

"Okay." Caden frowned, clearly not seeing a problem with this. "We probably should coordinate with him about--"

"He took the idea and ran with it," she cut him off.

Valerius pinched the top of his nose. He had thought that by sending Marban to the ends of the Earth to get people for the Shifter Council that he would be out of Valerius' hair. But no, no, of course not.

"All right." Caden was still not seeing a problem clearly. "So what--"

"He's already announced it," she continued quickly. "And he's making it like a joint thing and--"

At that moment, Chione came out of the castle doing one of her fast walks that meant she'd seen something she had to tell him about or show him. He did not keep a phone on him often. He liked to avoid the news like the plague. She made him acknowledge some of it.

"Valerius, you best see this," Chione was saying as she thrust her tablet at him.

At the same time, Rose said, "He's told everyone that Iolaire will be there *today*. Like in a few hours. As his special guest!"

Valerius saw the same announcement running on the news that Iolaire would be exclusively appearing in the Below with Marban at two that afternoon. Kaila was suddenly at his shoulder, edging Chione out.

"Oh, that looks fun!" Kaila enthused. "I want to go!"

THE RULE

"*T*ell me why I shouldn't kill you, Marban?" Valerius said to the smirking--it wasn't a grin, it was a smirk!--Swarm Shifter who stood like a supplicant in front of him.

Valerius had told Chione to summon Marban from the Below and have him marched to the throne room. No cozy meeting in his quarters. No come at his convenience. It was come now, bring Rose, and not to speak until spoken to. He'd sent Rose immediately to Caden. So Marban would feel the full weight of his fury!

Except Marban seemed not to feel that weight at all but was now smiling benignly at Valerius, seeming as happy to meet in the throne room as anywhere else. Maybe he hadn't been smirking earlier either. It was hard to go from enemy to ally without some kind of carry over belief that the person was trying to still get one over on you.

But he has gotten one over me! He is trying to use Caden and Iolaire for his own personal gain! To burnish his new found respectability a little more...

If we send a fire stream at him, the bug will sizzle and snap! Raziel added his growl as it looked at Marban's Spirit form in the mirror.

In that mirror, the room appeared filled with a swarm of wasps who flew like one entity, forming elaborate shapes in the air.

The human form of Marban spread his hands wide and the wasps formed what looked like two giant wings.. The sleeves of his monk's robes--for gods' sake, he was wearing *monk's* robes to accentuate the idea he was a wise and kind--fell back as he did so. "My king, I am uncertain why you are angry with me. I thought that you would be thanking me."

"T-thanking you!" Valerius sputtered.

Fire erupted from Raziel's mouth as it, too, could not believe the Swarm Shifter's gall. Chione, who was standing to his right side, gently pressed a hand on his shoulder. She didn't want to see him use hellfire again that day. Really, it was going to take ages to fix the dungeon. If he destroyed the throne room as well... No, he would keep his temper.

"Indeed," Marban answered with another benign smile and no fear whatsoever. Either he thought he was in no danger or he had ice water in his veins. Likely a little bit of both. Valerius wasn't a murderer... not anymore in any case. And Marban had weathered the storms of his temper before. "The children had this plan." He chuckled indulgently. "And, while their hearts were in the right place, the plan wasn't very... well, *good*."

"Caden and Rose only had a *shadow* of an idea! But then you came, heard Rose's hopes for it and set a *date*! A *time*! You sent out *press releases*! You are selling *merchandise*! So do not blame this on the children!" Valerius roared.

"But they were going to do it no matter what I did." Marban tented his fingers together. "And they were going to do it *without* telling you. You did just find out about it now, correct?"

Valerius gave Marban a death stare. That was true. Caden had sputtered out this shadow of a plan to him after the phone call with Rose ended. They hadn't really figured it out yet! They were working on it! They would have told him... eventually. If they thought it wouldn't make him mad. And that he wouldn't say no. Okay, so maybe they wouldn't have told him and would have asked forgiveness afterwards. Caden had then given him puppy eyes, which had Tez melting, Esme looking indulgent and Kaila petting Caden's head and saying, "Nice puppy Dragon."

Valerius had then sent Caden with the others to Esme's rooms. Caden was *not* to go anywhere until after Valerius had interrogated Marban. Except it seemed that Marban was interrogating *him*. Or, at least, Marban was asking the questions.

"Yes, I can see that is true." Marban nodded sagely. "So I knew that they would do this and would not tell you and, of course, make a *mess.*"

"So you made it a bigger mess? I'm failing to see where the thanking should be coming in," Valerius retorted dryly as he shifted in his throne. The long black fur coat slid over his leather pants.

"On the contrary, I have made sure it will work," Marban insisted. "Rose was so *hopeful* that this would bring awareness of some of the problems in the Below to the wider world. The White Dragon comes there to play with the children, being unafraid of a Swarm Shifter, and treats the people in the Below as... well, *worthy* as everyone else at attention."

Valerius squeezed the top of his nose. He felt a headache coming on. This sounded exactly like Caden and Rose. Well, more like Caden than Rose. She was far more practical. But Caden seemed to be bringing out the romantic in her too.

"Seems you are not alone in softening under Caden's influence," Chione whispered into his ear.

"I think Caden drives us all a little insane. In a good way." Valerius' lips were twitching suspiciously as he said it. His ill humor even with Marban could not defy Caden's effect on him.

But he hardened his exterior as he addressed Marban quite frostily, "You are not doing this for the people of the Below. You are doing this for yourself. That is why you have written in permanent marker your name all over this good deed Caden and Rose intended."

Marban shrugged, but he made it seem like a kingly gesture as if he were giving more than receiving. "I merely used my resources to make that gesture so much more. Did you know they weren't even going to tip off the news beforehand? How foolish!"

"I am certain that they intended to make the people of the Below feel special, but not to make it a press event," Valerius replied frostily.

"Yes, but, again, how wasteful! My actions will help increase the good effects of their actions! You can only do a thing once," Marban scoffed. "A second or third visit won't mean as much if they wish to draw attention to the poverty and desperation of our most power-less citizenry. It will encourage others to do something about that plight."

"You are the one that keeps the status quo in the Below as it is, Marban. It is how you secure your power. If people had options, they would not choose to follow you." Valerius tapped the arm of his throne in irritation. "You act as if you could not change the fates of those people in the Below, as if you are an observer, when we both know that you could make a positive impact in their lives."

The Swarm Shifter's eyes narrowed. "I *do* make a positive impact, my king, but I must work within the rules. Not even I am above them."

"What rules are you speaking of, Marban?" Chione asked, clearly interested in spite of herself.

Marban smiled again benignly. "My dear Chione, you know them well. We all know them well, though we do not name them often. The very first of these is simply this: that there must be those on top and those on the bottom."

"And you have taken advantage of that alleged rule to be on top of those on the bottom," Valerius replied dryly. "And you do that by keeping them desperate."

"I have clawed my way to the top of that very modest hill, yes," Marban admitted. "But *you*--you, dear King Valerius--are on top of the mountain that looms over my hill. Could I not say that you keep things as they are--the status quo--far more than I do?"

Valerius said nothing. Marban had a point.

Marban continued, "But I do not think it is within your power to *fix* the situation in the Below even as it is not within *mine*, King Valerius, because the rule holds sway. That is how it has been, is now, and always shall be."

"That is such a grim outlook," Chione murmured and her beautiful face was fixed in a frown.

"But you are a realist, too, Chione! You know what I say is true. In fact, I would guess that you see what I do," Marban said.

"Which is?" she asked.

"That it is getting worse. Or rather, there used to be many more in the middle. The top is still occupied by the few, but the bottom… well, the number is growing at the bottom," Marban pronounced.

Valerius cast a look at his Councillor. This was something they had spoken of often since Caden had come on the scene. With the exposure of Shifters, the world had changed in many ways, but perhaps the most unexpected to all of them, were how the humans were being squeezed out.

It was inevitable with the resources that Shifter had: immortal life, eternal youth, greater strength and speed, near indestructibility, wisdom of the ages, and unlimited wealth. All humanity had on its side was the ability to have children and a sense of urgency that immortality slowly stripped away.

Unless they implemented some kind of system that required a certain amount of humans in jobs, humans would be relegated to the lowest work or no work. But the political will was not there. Humans didn't want "charity" as President Goodfellow had told him, they wanted to be "respected" for what they did bring. But what they did bring to many jobs was just not enough anymore.

Caden would argue that I am not seeing the value of human thought and other aspects of humanity, Valerius thought. *Maybe he is right. But no one else is seeing it. Caden's father would be quick to tell him how many people won't hire human lawyers any longer when they have an option to hire a Raven Shifter. Justice. St. John would think it imprudent to have a judge who did not have several hundred years under his or her belt to decide cases. Human soldiers would be ripped apart by Werewolves before they could get a shot off. And human police officers cannot go up against Shifter criminals. It's just too dangerous.*

Marban's words pulled him from those dark thoughts, "But Caden is the antidote to that."

"How so?" Valerius asked, wondering what insane scheme Marban had built in his mind around the youngest of the Dragon Shifters.

Marban smiled thinly. "He gives hope."

That word "hope" hung in the air like frost for a moment. Valerius almost laughed. Caden created delight. He caused wonder. He was a joy to be with. But hope? What did Marban mean by that? Hope seemed something that the Swarm Shifter would have little time for.

"Of course," Chione murmured. She tapped her chin. "If you believe that becoming a Shifter means a better life--"

"It does. And even for those such as myself..." Marban looked at the swirling swarm of insects in the glass that would have terrified a farmer down to their bones. "Even for those of us not quite as *lucky* in terms of what type of Shifter they become, there are still advantages from simply being human. But Caden is so much more than that. He went from being--well, not the lowest--but from the middle to the top. The very, very top."

"The people don't know who Iolaire's human counterpart is," Valerius said, knowing that Caden intended to change that. "They have no idea about his background.

"Oh, but they will. How long can that be kept secret?" Marban raised a hairy eyebrow. There were longer strands of hair that stuck out from his forehead more like whiskers than eyebrows. "Too many people know. There is video evidence. It is inevitable. He will be exposed. And I do so hope you decide to manage how that information comes out."

"Will that be a good thing or a bad thing when they know?" Chione asked.

"Oh, a good thing for the status quo," Marban told her. "Because that *thinning* middle is really where the danger lies more so than the bottom. If the middle loses hope then... Well, that's when the revolution begins."

"You're saying that Caden represents hope to humanity because he shows that anyone--but, more importantly, someone this middle can relate to, someone they could be--could join the highest ranks of the Shifters?" Chione carefully articulated.

"Yes, exactly." Marban laced his fingers together behind his back and began to walk back and forth from the mirror to the open doors of the courtyard and back again. The swarm of wasps swooped and turned as he did in the mirror. "Caden means that they are not *stuck*. That things are not *set*. That there is still a chance for them under the *current* system to get higher, therefore--"

"There is no need to change it?" Valerius finished the sentence for him.

Marban smiled and nodded. "So Caden is the hope you see. He is the old American dream."

"So that's why..." Chione whispered, a flash of horror on her face.

And Valerius knew what she was thinking. That was why the Faith were doing this. They believed their only hope--their only salvation-- was to become Shifters in the long run. They believed the status quo would be how things were forever so they had to go from the bottom to the top. Or from the middle to the top.

Caden is proof of that. Or what they perceive as truth.

Suddenly, Valerius did not want to sit on this throne any longer. He felt hemmed in by this massive room with its ornate magic mirror and stone walls. He wanted to fly away from all of this with Caden at his side. He didn't want to be the cause of people blowing each other up to try and become Shifters. He didn't want to think of the desperation that had to be growing in those hearts to think such a thing was the answer.

Before the top meant being rich. Now it means being a Shifter. Humans First could not be behind this bombing based upon that very fact. And Shifters randomly would not do this. No, no, it has to be the Faith...

Marban had paused in his pacing when Valerius rose. The Swarm Shifter was studying their faces.

"You know something," Marban intuited. "What do you know?"

"I'm surprised that you don't already know it yourself, but you haven't had your ear to the ground here as you've been traveling," Valerius said.

He had expected the Swarm Shifter to know of Serai's death and the rebellion of the robots. But perhaps he hadn't had a chance to talk to his spies in the castle yet since he was too busy arranging Caden's appearance in the Below.

"What have I missed?" Marban was practically quivering.

"We need a drink for this," Valerius said.

He gestured for Marti to get some wine. He needed wine. And then he stalked outside where the table where their breakfast had been laid out was. Marban and Chione followed after him. He stood at the edge of the wall looking down at the city.

"You are going to tell him?" Chione asked softly as Marti opened the red wine and poured it into three glasses.

"You do not think it wise?" Valerius asked.

Marban was giving them the illusion of privacy. He stood by the table, swirling and sipping the wine like a true connoisseur. Valerius was half tempted to ask him if had any Ambrosia on him. But now, above all, was not the time to get drunk.

"Marban has no love for the Faith," she said.

In fact, Marban had a great hatred towards them. At least Valerius thought so based on how Marban shooed out of the Below all the do-gooders. The Faith always wanted to go into the Below and preach their religion, but Marban never allowed it for long. Valerius had always believed that it was because Marban, alone, wanted to be the one who was the giver of gifts to the Below.

"Marban, what do you know about the Faith?" Valerius asked without turning around.

Marban handed one of the glasses of wine to Chione as he answered, "I find them to be menaces."

"Because they undermine your power?" Valerius asked as Marban offered him a glass.

"You always do go to the heart of the matter." Marban was smiling as he said it. "Thou shalt have no god before me."

"God?" Chione's eyebrows rose.

Marban bowed to her. "No, no, dear lady, I am hardly a god, but what I mean is simple: I do not want divided loyalty. Religious people always put their religion above all else usually."

"It might be good that you kept them out," Valerius murmured before downing the entire glass of wine.

Marban cocked his head to the side as his eyes narrowed. "You *definitely* know something. I am intrigued and a little alarmed."

"We think we know who is behind the bombings," Chione answered. "Though, if we are right, I am not sure how to defend against them."

"The Faith..." Marban guessed. His expression went from thoughtful to angry. "Of course, it would be them!"

"They know the rule, Marban. But they see the top as Shifters, not only because Shifters are dominating every profession and so much more," Chione said, "but also because they believe Shifters are... well, *gods*."

"Zealots," Marban hissed. "That is not good."

"No, it is not," Valerius agreed.

Marban grabbed the bottle and refilled their glasses. Valerius hadn't been the only one to drink theirs down.

"You cannot offer someone something greater than their religion offers," Marban stated. "That kind of belief is very difficult to shake, especially now when Shifters are right here. No longer do you have to have faith. Proof of what you believe is all around you."

"Exactly," Valerius said, cradling his drink against his chest.

He had only really thought of how Caden revealing his identity would affect the young man. Not how it would affect others. Caden would be a symbol of what was possible. Would people be blowing themselves up in the hopes that they would join the top? He shut his eyes. Feeling dizzy and sick.

"I was always glad that you never were as in love with the Faith. But you've allowed them to continue on," Marban stated, his lips writhing back from his teeth. He reminded Valerius of a Rat Shifter rather than a Swarm Shifter.

"Freedom of religion is something guaranteed in Valerius' territory," Chione responded with a little fire in her demeanor. "People who believe are not dangerous."

"So long as they do not act on those beliefs and decide to blow people up in the hopes of creating more Shifters," Marban retorted.

"Caden's own mother is a member of the Faith, and I am certain that she would *never* blow people up," Chione answered.

"But Serai did," Valerius interrupted the argument. "And others will too."

"Bringing the ninth Dragon Shifter into the world will just add to that zealotry," Marban muttered.

"We saw another explosion at the Humans First meeting, but thankfully, there were no deaths," Chione stated. "Is that why they haven't done more?"

"They cannot be sure that the bomb created the ninth Dragon Shifter," Valerius stated. "Caden hasn't told his story. Perhaps they need confirmation before they truly get going. After all, the ninth Dragon Shifter could have simply been hiding all this time. Though why they would, I do not know."

"Because Caden *is* going to tell his story," Chione said, a look of growing horror on her face again.

"Yes," Valerius agreed. Despair wanted to well within him.

"Should we tell him not to?" Chione asked. "Should we tell him to lie if he does?"

All of these were good questions. All of them were things he hadn't considered. They added a level of complexity that was almost mind numbing. And all of it would be on Caden's shoulders even though Valerius would tell him that it was not his fault what others did.

At that moment, Simi came out onto the courtyard. His eyes slid to Marban for a moment, and a flicker of disgust crossed over his handsome features, before he bowed low and said, "The Bryces are here, my king. They are demanding to see their son. And they've brought a boatload of lawyers with them."

TERRITORY

"What do you suppose they're talking about? Valerius and Marban?" Caden asked Rose.

She was tense as a bow beside him. "You think Valerius is saying anything? I'm wondering if I'll have a grandfather left after Valerius shreds him or uses that hellfire on him that you told me about!"

They were standing together on Esme's balcony with Esme and Tez seated at one of the garden tables a little way down from them. Kaila was on the other side of them, leaning over the balcony railing so far that her bare feet had left the ground.

"They are too far away to hear." Kaila was leaning over the railing and craning her neck. "Can't see them either."

"They are in the throne room, dear. Valerius is impressing upon Marban the full weight of his kingship," Esme answered as she continued her scan of Serai's electronic communications, still searching for the conspirators behind the bombings. "But knowing Valerius' feelings about Marban, I am certain the subject of death, throttling, burning to a crisp and the like came up."

"I know!" Kaila was kicking her feet, rather like she was treading water, but instead was treading only air, as she tried to somehow see the throne room. Caden resisted the urge to pull her back. If she fell off she'd just shift into her Dragon form. But still, he felt a little sick watching her teeter. "That's why I want to hear and see! I am betting it is an epic beatdown."

"He is a Swarm Shifter. Locusts, I believe. Is it locusts, Rose?" Esme asked.

She nodded, biting her lower lip until it nearly bled.

"Well, then, it cannot be much of a beatdown. One breath of fire and the insects would be instantly destroyed," Esme said coolly as she swiped and read.

Rose's chin rose up. "Swarm Shifters aren't without the ability to fight!"

"She didn't mean it like that, flower girl," Kaila said, still teetering. "Even I have heard of this Marban out on the water. He is sly and clever and there are more ways to fight than physically, which is a good thing because few creatures can stand before a Dragon and survive."

Rose swallowed and went pale even though Kaila was complimenting Marban. She balled one hand and brought it down on the railing. "I shouldn't have said *anything* to Marban! If I had just stayed quiet none of this would have happened!"

"You are not responsible for any of this, Rose. Stop beating yourself up," Caden told her. He reached over and covered her balled hand with his on the balcony railing.

"But I *am* responsible, Caden! Marban wouldn't have known anything about our plan but for me! But I..." She looked so miserable that his heart hurt and Iolaire twittered softly. "I told him because I thought he would be--oh God--*proud* of me. That since he was being civic-minded himself that he would see that I was trying to improve things for the Below. But I forgot." Her mouth twisted like she was tasting something sour. "He's only in this for *himself*. Unless he can take advantage of it, it doesn't matter."

Caden tended to agree with her. "Yeah, that's what I think about Marban, too, but just because he wants in on it, doesn't mean it's a bad idea. In fact, him wanting to be a part of this means it's a *great* idea."

Her wrenched expression softened a little. "I suppose it does. Marban doesn't try to take ownership of bad plans."

"No, I bet he doesn't." Caden grinned at her.

She bit her lower lip though. "Yeah, okay, so maybe the plan is good and Marban wanting to get in on it isn't absolutely terrible, but Valerius finding out this way..."

Caden scrubbed the back of his neck with his right hand. "He will get over it. Eventually. Maybe in a millennia."

"Oh, Caden, I'm so sorry!" Rose cried.

"Don't worry! It will be all right." Caden hoped that as much as believed it. Maybe hoped a little more than he believed.

Tez, who was fishing out the grapes from a cup of fruit cocktail-- and Caden wondered where he'd gotten that--answered, "He should not be angry at you at all, Caden. You are both trying to help the least powerful of us. That is a noble endeavor. More of our kind should do so."

"You said *should* not, Tez, which means you think he will be," Caden pointed out.

Tez, after chewing a grape contemplatively, answered, "Yes, because Valerius is not a man of the people. It's not that he doesn't like poor people and prefers rich people."

"No, he is not fond of people in general," Caden agreed with him. "So he's an equal opportunity disliker."

"Exactly!" Tez fished out another grape. He gazed at it almost lovingly then popped it in his mouth. "That is why you will have to bear some of his wrath, Caden. You like people and want to be out among them. He thinks they are nothing but trouble."

"People are trouble." Kaila turned from surveying the city. "But that's what makes them fun. I think your idea to appear in the Below is a good one and you should do it."

"I think Valerius may have something to say about that." Esme looked over the top of her tablet at Kaila with a small smile.

Kaila put her hands on her hips and scowled at the Blue Dragon Shifter. "Is Caden not a Dragon Shifter?"

"Of course, dear," Esme answered.

"So he is our equal, yes?" Kaila pressed.

"*Our* equal? Yes, he is, of course." Esme smiled faintly. It was a smile that said Kaila was walking straight into her trap.

"Then Caden can go and meet the people if he wants to!" Kaila smacked her right hand down on Caden's left shoulder.

"Ah, but you have forgotten *one* thing." Caden could almost hear Esme's trap snapping shut as the Blue Dragon Shifter said, "While Caden is *our* equal, none of us are *Valerius'* equal."

Both his and Kaila's shoulders slumped as they both realized the import of what she was saying. Rose sighed and shook her head.

"She is right," Tez sighed. "Valerius is the first among equals though he is usually loath to assert his authority."

"Not anymore. Or, at least, not about you, Caden," Esme replied. "He is very involved."

Caden colored. "Well, he's--he's protective of me because I'm new."

"New? Hmmm, he was never like that with you, Tez, when you were new, was he, dear?" Esme turned to Tez.

Tez looked almost startled. "What? No! I believe the first time we met he shouted at me." Tez sniffed. "And scowled. It upset Eldoron greatly."

Caden's lips wanted to twitch into a smile, but he pressed them tightly together so he didn't upset Eldoron too. Rose covered a snicker by turning it into a cough.

"And, Kaila, was Valerius protective of you when your Spirit bonded with you?" Esme asked.

Kaila shrugged. "I don't remember. It was more important to speak to my dolphin friends than him."

"So that is likely a *no*." Esme sighed.

Caden's cheeks flamed hotter and he looked at the ground. "Maybe he just thinks I need more help than you guys did."

"Caden!" Rose shook her head in faint exasperation. "Marban said that the moment he saw the two of you together that there was something more there."

"Marban said that?!" Caden's eyes went huge.

"Anybody who has ever seen the two of you together says that!" Rose laughed.

"I didn't know it was so obvious. Things have just..." Caden blushed but pushed out, "gotten more serious recently."

"Other than the Dragon fighting, it seemed like you guys were pretty tight from the very beginning. That night on the bridge, he picked you up and flew off with you," Rose reminded him.

"That was to get me out of trouble." Caden was scrubbing the back of his neck again, which had also turned bright red he was sure.

Tez seemed fascinated by Caden's blushes. He had abandoned his fruit cocktail--or maybe there were no more grapes--and was sitting on the edge of his seat, all agog. "Caden, are you and Valerius... *mates?*"

Caden immediately thought of Iolaire and Raziel, how their heads were *nearly* touching as if they were inhabiting one body instead of two.

"Tez!" Esme chastened. "You do not ask that!"

"Well, how are we to know if we do not ask?" Tez challenged her.

"You need to be told?" Kaila looked bewildered.

"It is better than making assumptions!" Tez's voice was high.

Kaila rolled her eyes. "If you must be told then you must be quite blind."

"I would not be *asking* at all if I were *blind*." Tez scowled at her.

"We haven't--haven't discussed it," Caden said quickly, which was true.

"Do you need to discuss it, dear?" Esme gave him a knowing smile.

He lowered his head again. "It's just starting."

"Yes," Esme nodded. "But I will tell you something, I have *never* seen Valerius with anyone like he is with you."

Tez eagerly nodded, too. "Yes, he is not romantic! As I said before, Valerius does not like people!"

"But he likes you, Dragon puppy." Kaila patted his cheek.

"I am not a Dragon puppy!" Caden laughed.

"You are! Those *eyes*," Kaila giggled. "And you're so cute."

"I like Valerius, too. Very much. Very, very much."

What he didn't say was that who Iolaire liked was far more important. Caden was along for the ride. That doubt--that niggling doubt--that he was just an accident surfaced again in full force. He felt like an imposter all of a sudden.

He was certain that Iolaire and Raziel were mates. But him and Valerius? He knew what his heart said. It said *yes*. But that was because he *wanted* it to be true. But mates meant being fated and perfect for one another and all of that. Yet how could that be if he wasn't meant to be with Iolaire in the first place? Iolaire tilted its head at him, no comprehension on its face. It twittered at him lovingly.

I love you, too, Iolaire, but be honest with me. Did you choose me because I was your chance to be with Raziel? Raziel is your mate. I know that.

You, Iolaire said.

What about me? Caden asked back, amused and not understanding at the same time.

I am you. You are me, Iolaire said.

Caden's forehead furrowed. *Only because I was going to be blown up. You saved me!*

You saved me, Iolaire mirrored his words.

But it was an accident that brought us together, Caden objected.

Always meant to be together. Always, Iolaire said.

Always? You mean you would have found a way to bond with me? Caden asked.

Yes. Always. Iolaire blinked softly at him like a cat does when saying they loved the person they were looking at.

"Caden, you okay?" Rose touched his shoulder.

Caden blinked. He felt like he was coming out of deep water. He shook himself and then started to smile. "Y-yeah, I was just talking to Iolaire."

The smile grew so broad that his cheeks hurt. Iolaire flapped its wings happily.

"O-okay," Rose laughed uncertainly at his sudden, brilliant, beaming happiness.

"I was just... I don't know. Doubting myself," he told her and then

96

glanced around at the other Dragon Shifters. "Meeting you guys has been amazing, but it's also daunting. I thought maybe Iolaire made a mistake by choosing me. Or it was an accident. Or just a convenience because I was there."

"Oh, my goodness, Caden!" Esme looked so sad at him. "That's not how this works! Spirits have one person that they are meant for. The moment we come together with them is when we are ready."

"But the mate thing... doesn't that complicate things?" Caden's cheeks, which had been red before, were now nuclear in heat and color. They didn't know about how Iolaire and Raziel were now able to be seen together as if they occupied one body instead of two. There was only a thin line separating them. "I mean, it's not just me and Valerius in this, but Iolaire and Raziel!"

"Truly? Your Dragons are mates, too?" Tez's mouth was open.

Esme looked at him quizzically. "Tez, dear, why *wouldn't* their Dragons be involved in this mating business? Humans don't have fated mates."

Tez flushed. "Well, Eldoron is rather particular about the idea of sex--"

"You and your Dragon talk about sex?" Rose interrupted.

"Well, Eldoron is very beautiful so it has many suitors." Tez sniffed and rubbed the fingernails of his right hand against his shirt.

"But you came here to *court* Caden," Rose pointed out.

Tez blinked rapidly. "I came to show off Eldoron's loveliness and my considerable charms."

"You both are wonderful," Caden said kindly.

"But like in everything else, Valerius is the first among equals." Esme twinkled at him.

"If you are Valerius' mate then you must show you are his equal!" Kaila stomped her foot.

"Uhm, how would I do that?" Caden tilted his head to the side, knowing already that Kaila got into trouble even more than he did.

"By having your time with the people! We will go now!" Kaila grabbed Caden's right wrist and Rose's left wrist and started to drag them towards the front doors of Esme's suite. "We will convince Valerius that you can do as you like!"

The moment Esme's guards opened the door they were unable to go forward, because Illarion was standing there. He wore a tailored blue serge suit with an icy white shirt flared open at the collar. His hands were slid negligently into his pants pockets and he looked freshly showered. Illarion's eyes narrowed as he took in Rose. They narrowed more as he took in Kaila.

"I thought I smelled *fish* earlier," Illarion said to Kaila.

"And I thought I smelled *dung*," Kaila answered.

"What are you doing here, Illarion?" Caden found himself asking. "I thought for sure you'd have packed your things and headed home by now."

Rose cast a nervous glance at him. Her eyes were slightly wide as she realized who this was: Dragon King Illarion, the Green Dragon, the Poisoner. And here Caden was treating him like he was no one important.

Illarion took a moment too long to answer to show Caden's words had affected him, but he then smoothly asked, "Why would I do that?"

"I'm not a girl, remember?" Caden's voice was tart.

Rose's head jerked between them. "He thought you were a girl? Why?"

"Evidently, Iolaire is too comely and graceful to be a boy," Caden said without his gaze leaving Illarion's face.

"You're kidding, right?" Rose asked, her voice low as if Illarion couldn't hear her.

"Unfortunately, no," Caden answered her. "So why are you still here, Illarion? There's nothing for you here. There would be nothing for you even if I were a girl by the way."

"But we hardly know one another!" Illarion said. "You have only heard others' opinions of me."

"Yeah, but what I hear is universally bad," Caden retorted. "And the first time I met you, you were flying in Valerius' territory without permission. We had to take you down."

Again, there was that stiffness in Illarion's form, which told Caden that he was angry at Caden's words, but pretending not to be. He finally broke that stillness by chuckling uncomfortably. Illarion's smile was more of a rictus.

"Yes, well, I was just trying to remind Valerius that he is not above us," Illarion said.

"Funny, as everyone else was just telling me that he is above all of you. The king of kings. The first among equals." Caden crossed his arms over his chest.

Illarion let out a bark of laughter. "Of course, they do! They are sheep! I am not. And I do not think..." Illarion's eyes narrowed, "I do not think you are either, Caden. So I am *not* leaving. I am *staying* to get to know you better."

Illarion moved to take Caden's arm and lead him back into Esme's rooms. She had appeared in the threshold of the balcony doors with Tez following after her.

"Well, *we* are leaving," Kaila informed Illarion, having remained silent, but fuming as Illarion had talked. "So you need to get out of the way."

Kaila was as tall as Illarion and the two of them were practically pressed nose to nose at that moment.

Illarion's nostrils flared. "You are in my way, Kaila. There is nothing that you could want Caden for that is more important than I do. There are no *fish* here for you to speak to."

Kaila's nose wrinkled as if Illarion smelled bad. "I think Caden would better like to speak to fish than to *you*."

Rose tugged his hand. "Maybe we should get out of here while the getting's good."

Kaila and Illarion had started to circle one another. For a moment, Caden imagined the Green Dragon and the Turquoise Dragon in their places. Wings would be flapping angrily. Massive mouths open to expose teeth. Poisonous smoke billowing from Illarion's jaws. The power of the sea reflected in Kaila's eyes.

"You might have the right idea," Caden said as he took a step back towards the open doors.

"I thought you would want to step in and bring peace," Rose

remarked as they both turned and hustled out the door, leaving Tez and Esme actually urging Kaila and Illarion to fight.

"Uhm, no, no, not really. I figure the more times that Illarion is trounced, the better things are in the world," Caden admitted as they hustled down the hallway.

"Why, Caden, I thought you were a peaceable Dragon!" Rose laughed. "You sound almost rational with this running away business!"

He grinned at her. "I think Kaila needs to let off some steam. That's probably one of her powers as she is another water Dragon. Seriously, though, we should go talk to Valerius and Marban about what we want to do in the Below. Kaila was right about that. But I think she sort of gets on Valerius' nerves."

"Because she's not impressed with him?" Rose smirked.

"How did you guess that?"

"She doesn't seem impressed by anyone."

They hustled down the stairs and headed towards the throne room. Even before they neared the side doors, Caden could hear raised voices coming from inside. He and Rose exchanged worried glances. They slowed just as they came to the side doors. Without speaking, both stopped just out of sight and listened. Caden had expected to hear Valerius' gruff growl and Marban's calming one. But that was *not* who was speaking.

"King Valerius, I demand to see my son," his father's voice rose up.

"Oh, my God, *Dad*?" Caden whispered. "What is he doing here?"

Rose shook her head in confusion. They both continued to listen.

"It was my understanding that you were the one not speaking to Caden," Valerius actually sounded reasonable. He was keeping his temper despite Caden's father's tone.

"We had an argument and I let my temper get ahead of me. I think *you* can appreciate that," his father said tightly. "But though my son thinks he can do everything on his own, he cannot. He needs help. Especially with all of the Dragons here trying to stake their claim to him like that Illarion creature."

"He is not alone," it was Marban who spoke, which had Caden and

Rose exchanging shocked glances. Marban and Valerius were working together! "We are all here to assist Caden in making the right choices."

"Who are you?" His father snapped. "Oh, yes, you're that gangster! You have criminals by your side, King Valerius? Criminals who seek to get their claws into my son!"

Caden pinched the top of his nose.

But though his father had meant to insult Marban, the wily, old Swarm Shifter seemed completely unmoved by it, "Mr. Bryce, there is something you should know about becoming a Shifter. It places each of us in a certain sphere. As a Swarm Shifter, my sphere was not so exalted. I made the best of it. But even though Caden has joined the highest of the high, he will need the wits I learned at the bottom."

Rose bit her lower lip again. Her gaze was inward. What was she thinking? That she was in the lowest sphere? She wasn't. She was here with him and she had every right to be. He reached over and touched her shoulder. She lifted her head and focused on him. She seemed to know what he was thinking. She smiled, but faintly.

"I have some wit myself," his father said.

"Oh, yes, top of your class at Harvard Law School," Marban listed off. "You apprenticed with Justice Whyler of the Second Circuit. You wrote several influential papers. And then you became a partner at your firm."

"Yes, I did," his father sounded less certain all of a sudden.

"But I am betting that despite all of your accomplishments that this is the most sure of yourself you've been in a long time. Perhaps this is the most respect you have ever had from your partners," Marban guessed, and Caden knew he guessed right.

"Marban always knows a person's weakness," Rose whispered.

"I have done good work," his father said, but weakly.

"Of course, you have. I didn't say you haven't. I spoke of certainty and respect!" Marban chuckled. "Those two things are so *rare* when you are down on the bottom. I know this. And, if you are honest with yourself, you know it too. So I speak to you as a fellow man whose talents and strengths have been *ignored* until recently."

"I never ignored you, Marban," Valerius said tightly.

"You are too kind to say so, my king," Marban answered. "But, like you, Mr. Bryce, my usefulness was not apparent to some people until Caden joined with his Spirit."

"I am not here for myself!" his father objected tersely. "I am here for my *son*. All the Dragons are coming here and, before they leave, I will have justice for Caden."

"What does justice look like in your eyes, Mr. Bryant?" Valerius asked.

"That Caden has his own territory so he is dependent on no one," his father answered and Caden grimaced.

Not this again!

"The other Dragons will not agree. It will cause war," Valerius told his father.

His father was not deterred by this as he said, "If that is true then will you agree to give him part of your territory, King Valerius?"

FIRED AND ICE

"$\mathcal{D}$ad," Caden's voice sounded surprisingly calm to Valerius considering the circumstances.

The moment the Black Dragon King sensed Caden and Rose in the hall, he had expected the young man to storm into the throne room and scream at his father. To rant and rave, in fact. Not to mention to remind Grant Bryce that he'd said "no" to a territory countless times before yet here Grant was demanding that Caden get what he didn't want. But Caden was completely calm. In fact, he sounded, if Valerius was going to put a name to it, *tired*. Maybe even *sad*.

As Caden and Rose emerged from the hallway and entered the throne chamber, Caden looked up at Valerius and gave a wave. Valerius found his mouth twitching into what suspiciously looked like a smile. Anytime he seemed to see Caden, he found his mood improving. Even when the young man was bringing trouble his way.

But the view of Thomas Storn and Leonard Guissler immediately squashed that happiness. The two lawyers were clearing their throats and shifting papers in their hands. They guessed there would be a family squabble in a moment despite Caden's gentle tone. They, undoubtedly, would like it to take place--if it had to at all--outside of

Valerius' view. They had no idea that Caden told Valerius most everything.

Unless it is some plan to go to the Below and get petted.

"Caden. Rose," Grant said both of their names fondly though there was the slightest tremor in it that human ears could not have heard.

"Dad, hey," Caden said, continuing in that calm and gentle manner as he went over to his father, completely ignoring the lawyers.

"Hello, Mr. Bryant," Rose said. She had her arms crossed over her chest. Her hands rubbed her own arms as if she were cold.

"My granddaughter *hurts* for them," Marban said from Valerius' left where he stood there as if he had always stood there.

There was an emotion in his voice that Valerius would not have thought possible: jealousy. Just a touch of it. Whatever Marban thought of his "grandchildren" and Valerius had always surmised it was not much, Marban, evidently, was not fond of them wanting to be a part of someone else's family.

"She sees the family that she wished she had," Valerius answered. "Having a... a *grandfather* only healed some of her pain."

"I doubt I healed any of it. Come now, Valerius, I take. I do not give," Marban answered quietly, but there was a look on his face as he watched Rose gaze with such concern at Caden and Grant that belied those words.

Chione stood on the opposite side of Valerius. In some ways, Valerius felt like he had an angel on one shoulder in Chione and a devil on the other in Marban. It should have felt strange to have Marban there with her. But it didn't.

Chione's hands folded together in front of her as she studied Caden's father. "Mr. Bryant is exhausted and desperate. He loves his son. He's not come here to do harm."

"Yes, but this is not the way to show it," Valerius answered her.

"No, but love is funny that way," she stated.

Grant Bryce stepped closer to his son so that he was almost invading Caden's space. He grasped Caden's biceps and held him at arm's length for long moments. Just looking at him as if to memorize Caden's face or see if there were differences.

Valerius noticed that Chione was right at that moment. Grant looked tired and worn. His worry about his son had been the one thing that had stopped Valerius from biting his head off figuratively and, maybe, literally. That and Caden being upset about it.

Grant embraced his son tightly. Caden's chin rested on his father's shoulder and Valerius could see Caden's expression. Caden's eyes closed for a moment. He loved his father quite deeply. That was what was making this all the more difficult for Caden. He had become a man after his father's death. He had never had to break from his father. So he could only imagine what Caden was going through. Caden's eyes opened at that moment and his gaze fixed on Valerius.

What do you want me to do, Caden? What can I do to help you? Valerius asked.

I'm not sure if you can do anything, Caden's voice came surprisingly clear. Their gift of communication was so spotty, but not now. *I sort of have a plan.*

Valerius' eyebrows lifted. *Famous last words, Caden.*

Caden grinned for a moment. *Yeah, I know, but I get why he's doing this now. He's scared.*

Yes, Valerius said. *I would imagine any father would be.*

And he's trying to control things, Caden added.

Understandable, Valerius agreed.

Just in the exact wrong way. Caden's smile dimmed.

Because of the fear.

It's like a snake eating its own tail, Caden sighed. *But, like I said, I think I have a plan.*

I would wish you good luck but... Valerius' eyes narrowed.

Don't worry! Well, you can worry, but since you're right here, even if I make a hash of it, things will be okay.

But Valerius knew that Caden had to do this on his own.

Caden pulled back and looked at his father. Grant stroked the sides of his son's head.

"Are you all right?" Grant asked.

"Yes, I'm fine," Caden assured him. "How are you? You don't look like you have gotten much sleep, Dad."

"I'm..." For a moment, Grant wavered slightly, which had Caden's eyes widening, but then Grant locked his knees. "I'm a little tired. We've been working on legal briefs all night and fine-tuning the arguments to be had with the Dragons."

"Arguments with the Dragons?" Caden let out a huff of laughter and pointed back the way they'd come. "Rose and I just left Kaila and Illarion squaring off in Esme's foyer."

"My money is on Kaila," Rose said with a quirk of a smile.

"Illarion is a monster! His idea of human rights is to put humans in camps!" Mr. Storn hissed.

"Yeah, Illarion is... something all right." Caden rubbed the back of his neck. "I guess what my point was is that I don't think they'll care about your arguments unless you have fire breath or water breath or... well, if you aren't a Dragon."

"All the more reason to secure your rights through the law," Mr. Guissler sniffed.

Caden grimaced. "Dad, I'm glad you're here."

His father's eyebrows lifted and a faint smile appeared on his face. "I admit I didn't expect to hear you say that. I expected a fight. Your mother was quite certain you would want nothing to do with me."

Caden smiled, but there was a sadness in that smile. "Well, she's not entirely wrong."

Grant stiffened slightly. But then Caden hugged him again quite fiercely. Grant softened against him.

"I love you so much, Dad," Caden breathed.

"And I love you, Caden. You are so important to me and I want what's best for you and--"

"And that's why I'm firing you as my attorney," Caden interrupted gently.

"What?" Grant froze.

"Now look here, young man!" Mr. Storn cried.

"I do say that you have the wrong end of things, Caden. We're here to protect your interests!" Mr. Guissler said.

"No, actually, you're here to protect your own and whatever my father wants for me." Caden pulled out of his father's embrace though he still kept hold of Grant's shoulders.

Grant looked like Caden had gutted him. Valerius took no pleasure in this, but he saw what Caden's plan was. It was a good one. It would hurt though.

"This is surprising and wise of the lad," Marban said, "though I do believe Mr. Bryce is not ready for it."

"He's been living in terror since Caden joined with his Spirit. All of his actions so far are because of that fear," Chione murmured with a shake of her head. "As a lawyer, he felt he could be in control of something, because as a father he was helpless. It wasn't just about how it helped *him*, Marban, as you suggested before."

Marban shrugged. "Perhaps not entirely. I am more used to the darker side of people than you, Chione. But what I see is a brilliant man who finally gets a chance to help a son he adores with the skills that have long been denied."

Valerius grimaced. He could see how those two things were likely driving Grant.

Caden continued, "Dad, I really do need you. I need your advice. I need your support. I need your love."

"Yes, that's what I'm trying to do. To be what you need," Grant said almost desperately. He did not understand why his son was firing him if Caden needed him.

"No, you're trying to do what *you* need." Caden gave him a wan smile. "I want you to be honest with yourself, if not with me, Dad. What is a lawyer supposed to do?"

Grant blinked and said uncertainly "Represent his client's best interests and--"

"No, actually, you've told me this yourself and that is that a lawyer *advises* a client as to what their best interests are, but after the client makes a decision--so long as it's not illegal--the lawyer assists them in getting that," Caden corrected. "Not what the lawyer thinks is best and certainly not what the client doesn't want. Right?"

Oh, Caden, I truly see what you are doing here, Valerius said sadly. *This will strip him of his last vestige of hope.*

I know. But I have to do it. I see now what's happening and I... I have to take control finally, Caden answered.

Grant looked flummoxed for a moment, but then knowledge flooded his expression. "Caden, it's because I'm your father, too, and I know you that I'm--"

"Going against my wishes?" Caden stared hard at him.

Color heated Grant's cheeks. "I'm trying to do what's best for you."

"As my dad, that's fine... though we need to talk about it. But as my *lawyer*? No lawyer acts against his client's desires, do they?" Caden pressed.

Grant's head lowered. "Caden--"

"No lawyer does that," Caden said quietly.

"Will he admit the truth of the boy's words?" Marban muttered, stroking his chin.

"He is a logical man. He will admit it. In time," Valerius said.

Grant put a hand to his right temple as if he was in pain there. "I want to keep you *safe*."

"You've got a wonderful mind, Mr. Bryce," Rose suddenly said. "A good head on your shoulders."

Grant turned to her. A wry smile on his lips. "But? I can tell you don't think I've been using those things in regards to Caden."

Rose lowered her head then lifted it and looked Grant in the eyes. "I told Caden that his parents would reject him as soon as they found out he was a Shifter."

Grant blinked. "I want to say that I cannot imagine any parent doing that. But I know it happens."

"It does. Far more often than you'd think. So, in truth, I never even considered what it would be like for a parent who *didn't* turn away," Rose said tentatively. Her hands laced together in front of her. Valerius could see her extreme discomfort in opening up this way, but she pressed on, "You love your son so much, and here he is with that big heart of his in the middle of... well, control of the world."

"No, Rose, I'm not--"

"Yes, Caden, you *are*. And the fact that you don't really get that a lot of the time is what is probably driving your father to distraction...

and Valerius too." Rose laughed softly when she saw Valerius nod. "Your good nature is a double-edged sword. It is the reason I feel--and I think so many people do--that it's *wonderful* that someone like you is in power. But it is also the reason why people fear for you so much. You don't see the bad in people even when they show you it."

Caden blinked and lowered his head. "Everyone makes mistakes. I can see how they got to the point they're at."

"Yes, exactly. You can put yourself in their shoes even when you would never do such a thing as they have done." Rose swallowed. "That's how you saw the good in me, even in Marban. That's why you have a grumpy Dragon over there allowing people to shout at him who should know better."

Grumpy Dragon? Valerius lifted an eyebrow at her. Rose pretended not to see.

"Mr. Bryce, I get it that you want to protect Caden, especially from himself." Rose gave a tremulous smile to Grant who returned it. "You're sick with worry. As a lawyer, and as someone who lived a little longer than Caden, you can see things ahead that he can't."

"Exactly!" Grant brightened. "That's why--"

"That's why you can't be his lawyer. Like Caden was saying. The truth is… Caden has got to make his own mistakes," Rose interrupted. "You can advise him, but you cannot take the choices away from him. And, believe me, there are so many things in the short time I've known your son that I wanted to stop him from doing, because I was *certain* they were bad ideas. Some of them were."

"Not all of them though!" Caden cried.

"Exactly. Not all of them. And those Caden gets right, they are *so* right," Rose explained. "You and I look and see dangers and problems and bad outcomes. Caden looks out and sees… opportunities. And the thing is, I believe, that it is *this* quality that makes you and I want to protect him from himself, that matches his Spirit. Caden is the ninth Dragon Shifter for a reason." Rose's hands had unclenched and she was reaching for Mr. Bryce. "You need to let him be who he is. Even if that means he makes mistakes, because some of those mistakes are going to teach him and others… others won't be mistakes at all."

Grant's reaction to Rose's words was to think deeply on them. His gaze went distant and he seemed to be listening to a voice inside of him. Caden looked like he wanted to hug Rose and spin her around. The two Raven Shifters were twitching like birds on an electrical line. Chione was openly crying. Valerius felt that in these words, that had been so difficult for Rose to say, that she had done more good than anyone.

"By the Gods, Marban, how did you not squash that young woman's spirit?" Valerius whispered.

"I like to think I nurtured it." Marban lifted his head.

"She's never going to stay your lackey," Valerius said. "Not anymore."

"No... but I will still have some of her heart," Marban said.

Valerius didn't doubt that was true. He feared it would cause Rose trouble down the line.

"If you feel your father is too close to this to represent you, you have both Mr. Storn and myself," Mr. Guissler said.

Grant came out of his thoughts instantly at their words. He shot them a look of betrayal and then his shoulders slumped. He slowly turned to Caden. "I think... I think you are right, Caden and Rose, that I am too close to this. And I've overstepped as an attorney, because... because I am your father. That may have deafened me to what you've been saying." With all of the dignity that he had remaining, Grant gritted out, "I would support you if you wished to hire Thomas and Leonard."

Caden immediately straightened and gave the two Raven Shifters looks of disgust. "No way! They've treated you terribly! Not just today, but like for *years*. I'm not rewarding them for that. And, Dad, you don't have to stay at their firm. If there's anything I want you to take advantage of with this Dragon Shifter stuff is that you should get a position that you deserve!"

Mr. Storn started to make a burbling noise. "N-n-now let's not be hasty--"

Mr. Guissler said at the same time, "Truly, emotions are high right now, Caden, but I can assure you--"

"Quiet!" Grant shouted. His face flamed with color, but then he added softer, "Quiet. My son and I are talking. The two of you... need to go. My son has said he doesn't want you as his attorneys. There's no further reason for you to be here."

"G-Grant? You can't be serious! You're our partner!" Mr. Storn cried.

Mr. Guissler's eyes narrowed. "Truly, Grant, you are being as emotional as your son! You should think things over carefully. You don't want to burn any bridges."

Grant laughed. It sounded high and shrill. "I could burn that bridge and salt the earth beneath it and you'd still keep me on as a partner or take me back. *Now*. So why don't we cut the crap. Both of you best get out of here."

"Grant, you're understandably stressed and tired," Mr. Guissler said with a toss of his head. "We'll speak later when you're rested. Come, Storn!"

With as much dignity as two puffed up birds could manage, the men strode out of the throne room. Silence fell.

Grant buried his face in his hands. Both Caden and Rose went to him.

"Dad, that was awesome!" Caden hugged his father fiercely while Rose patted his back awkwardly.

Grant groaned. "I do not know whether I will have a job tomorrow."

"Of course, you will," Marban said with a wheezy laugh. "What you said to them was true. But I think you should be more interested in what Caden said about your career."

"I think I'm done using my son's position to get me forward in my career." Grant kissed his son's forehead.

"Now who is being naive, Dad? You wanted me to have a whole territory, but you won't take a position that you can actually fill and do well in? Me as king of anything right now is... iffy," Caden said.

"Only *iffy*?" Rose's eyebrows lifted.

Caden--in a very kingly fashion--stuck his tongue out at her. But though everyone was smiling, Valerius was not. Because Grant Bryce had set a kind of bomb and it would go off unless...

Valerius began, "Caden, about the territory--about giving you some of mine--we should discuss it."

Caden looked up at him. "I would never expect you to give up territory to me, Valerius. I know that Dragons don't give up territory willingly--"

"You're actually considering it!" Grant looked shocked. "I never thought..."

Marban's eyebrows rose. "So people *can* surprise you."

"If Caden wants territory..." Valerius cracked his neck as the stiffness began. It was not *too hard* to say this. Raziel had been strangely silent this entire time and it would have to agree to truly give up some territory to Caden, but really considering how it felt about Iolaire... well...

"Valerius, I don't want to *take* anything from you. I won't. I want to *add* to what you have. Not take away!" Caden flapped his arms frantically. "I just want to be here with you and--"

"Oh my!" Chione gasped and every one gaped at her. She pointed to the mirror.

It was then that he caught movement in the mirror. When Valerius looked over, he saw Iolaire and Raziel reflected there. Their heads were moving towards one another's. He saw Iolaire flap its wings eagerly. Raziel's red eyes squinted with amusement and it let out a puff of fire. That was answered with a puff of frost. They rested their foreheads together.

Caden pointed at the two Dragons in the mirror. Unlike everyone else, Caden did not look surprised. "That's why I don't *want* or *need* territory. They have to be together. Nothing should separate them. Don't you see?"

Raziel let out another puff of fire and Iolaire met it with ice. The ice should have melted or the fire should have been cooled. But instead, the two swirled together and were equally sustained. Both Dragons closed their eyes in contentment.

Chione breathed, "So that's what fated mates looks like."

CIRCUS RING

"*A*m I really going to do this?" Caden asked Valerius.

"This *is* your plan, Caden." Valerius sounded amused.

"You could have talked me out of it!"

"After I saw how you and Rose handled your father, I knew I didn't have a chance." Valerius still sounded way too amused.

Caden twitched the huge black cloak with hood around his naked body. It was one of Valerius' *normal* cloaks that he wore when he traveled incognito in Reach. Caden was dwarfed by it. It pooled around his feet and he could have wrapped himself three times over and had material to spare. The hood hung all the way down to his chin unless he balanced it just so. It kept blocking his view of the Below's marketplace from their secret location behind a mostly broken down stall.

Well, it normally *was* the marketplace. In fact, it was where he had shifted and landed that first day he had joined with Iolaire. Now the area was completely transformed. The tin roofed stalls and piles of second-hand clothes and goods were all cleared away. The hard-packed earth was covered with a red carpet. That had Caden sighing. He knew that Marban had been behind it. It made Iolaire look more like a rockstar than a…

What? Normal Dragon? Okay, that's a little stupid. But it makes Iolaire look above the people and I don't want it.

But there had been no time to change it. After the confrontation with his father that had turned into a lot of hugging and a lot more honest talking and then hearing Kaila boast about how she had trounced Illarion--her wild hair and ripped clothes were worn with pride--he'd barely had time to travel with Valerius through the secret underground tunnels and pathways to the Below. He'd been awed by what he'd seen from spiraling staircases to sloping hallways carved with scenes of dragon battles.

"If you do not want to shift, Caden, Lana and I are well prepared to go in your stead!" Kaila looked at him brightly. She was balancing on her hoverboard with one hand firmly on Valerius' shoulder.

"I'm sure people would love to see you and Lana, but we promised them, uhm, Iolaire," Caden told her as he sheepishly tugged on the oversized hood. "Some people might be--*wrongly*--disappointed just because they were expecting something and got something else. Even if it is better!"

Kaila, who was still wearing the clothes that had gotten ripped in her *historic* battle with Illarion in Esme's foyer, which apparently was also the worse for wear, stuck her lower lip out in what suspiciously looked like a pout. But then she brightened again as her goldfish quick mind turned to something else.

"It's too bad that your father couldn't come with us!" she said.

Caden actually agreed. He still felt this utter sense of relief and comfort now that he and his dad were on the same page. In fact, he'd found himself wanting his father's opinion now that it wasn't being forced on him.

"While Caden intends to reveal himself, today is not the day. People are watching anything Iolaire is doing including those that attend its events in the hopes to track down anyone they consider suspicious," Valerius answered for him.

"Yes! Esme and Tez were looking at that online! They always spend so much time staring at screens that I--"

"Kaila, what were they seeing online about Iolaire?" Caden's forehead was furrowed. He had avoided looking for news about himself, but this must be important if Esme and Tez were interested in it. The two of them were still up in High Reach now, working with Mei on finding out more about who their real enemies were.

Kaila blinked as if she couldn't quite remember what she had been saying. Caden was about to remind her when she said, "Oh! Right! Well, there are whole YouTube channels dedicated to scanning the crowds where you've appeared. Also, they have video of the day of the bombing. That incident at your house is also being connected with everything going on."

Caden swallowed. He looked up at Valerius. "I am glad that I want to come out now. It doesn't seem like the secret could be kept much longer anyways."

Valerius nodded soberly. "I had a vain hope that we could keep your secret safe for a little time, but I doubt it will last the week. The thing is that none of us were joined with our Spirits during the Internet age."

"The Internet is wonderful! But it does have its drawbacks," Kaila agreed, but Caden had a hard time imagining her taking the time to sit still long enough to be on a computer or tablet or even a phone.

"But back to your father, Caden. His time is being well spent meeting with Justice St. John," Valerius said with a small smile.

"Dad acted like he was meeting a rockstar when the Justice appeared," Caden said with a faint huff of laughter.

His father had, in fact, totally geeked out in his lawyerly way when the head of the United States Supreme Court was announced. He then had gone almost silent when Valerius had introduced the two of them and the Chief Justice had actually known who he was.

"You clerked for Justice Whyler, didn't you?" St. John had asked his father.

"I--I did. I'm surprised that you would know about such a thing. It was a long time ago and I was one of many," his father answered.

"Justice Whyler is a friend of mine. He spoke of you often. He said you had a very strong forward thinking gift. You could see the results of a decision beyond the facts in front of you, which is very unusual," St. John had explained in that bone dry way of his.

"Unusual?" His father said the word as if it was bitter. Then with a keen-eyed stare, his father said, "You mean for a *human?*"

"No, Grant, for *anyone.*" St. John beamed at him.

His father blinked. Obviously, he was completely blown away by this. Caden hid his smile behind his hand.

"I hear that you are representing the White Dragon," St. John remarked.

His father's eyes did not even cut Caden's way as he answered, "No, I am not."

St. John's shrewd eyes narrowed. "And yet you are in the throne room of the king of kings."

"I am here on other business," his father half lied.

"Well, it is best not to involve home and work. The strains are simply too great. And our vision sometimes gets blurred by our emotions," St. John replied obliquely

Caden realized at that moment that the Chief Justice likely *knew* that Caden was the White Dragon Shifter, but was giving his father and Caden cover. Caden realized he never wanted to be on the opposite end of this man's questioning. He saw and understood way too much. His father's erect posture and stiff bearing indicated that he, too, knew that he was engaging with a master of verbal warfare.

"I noticed that some of your partners were storming out of the castle while I was coming in. No trouble there, I hope." St. John's head tilted birdlike to the side.

His father opened his lips to likely say "no" or "everything's fine" or, at the most, "there's only been a slight misunderstanding." But instead, his father said truthfully, "I believe I'm leaving the firm. We didn't see eye to eye on a lot of things."

St. John nodded sagely. "They are a good firm, but–if you will forgive me for saying this–slightly *pedestrian* in their pursuits. Now most firms are mostly conservative in order to serve their clients well, but they truly have lost the spark of creativity with the law. And I say this as a Supreme Court Justice whose life is to uphold what has come before, but, at the same time, we must look ahead. Something that, as I said, Justice Whyler said you could do."

His father narrowed his eyes for a moment then a smile curled his lips. "Justice St. John, are you trying to obliquely offer me a job?"

St. John put an arm around his father's shoulders. "I might be at that. As King Valerius is otherwise disposed, how about you and I discuss things?"

King Valerius had been warning staff to keep an eye out for Illarion since the Green Dragon Shifter's pride had been hurt and he was likely to do something stupid and dangerous.

"Caden, will you be all right if I go off with the Justice here for a moment?" his father asked with such a hopeful look that even if Caden had needed his father in that moment, he wouldn't have kept him.

"Go on, Dad. I've got a–a uh *thing* going on so I'm good." Caden waved him off.

Justice St. John's lips twitched faintly at his use of the word "thing". Yeah, the Chief Justice knew he was the White Dragon Shifter and clearly also knew about Marban's announcement. The two of them had wandered off together while Caden got ready for his big petting moment.

"I think Tilly, more than my dad, will have a cow when she hears about this," Caden remarked, drawing out of his thoughts.

"She already got her ride," Valerius growled.

"You aren't really worried that me giving some kids a ride will damage the fierce reputations of Dragons, are you?" Caden grinned up at him.

"If anyone ever asks me for a ride we shall know just how much *damage* you and Iolaire have done." Valerius' eyes blazed at him, but there was a smile tugging at the corners of his mouth.

"They would have to have a death wish to do that! But I suppose it could happen!" Kaila blew a curl away from her face as she leaned around the stall to peer at what was happening in the main circus ring as Caden was starting to call it in his head.

Marban had roped off a walkway that was near them, but did not lead right to their location, but close enough that they could slip into it without being noticed. The roping continued to form a huge circle right in the very center of the marketplace. The circle was large enough for Iolaire to sit, wings extended, to the delight of the crowd. And there was a huge crowd.

The entirety of the marketplace was filled. The crowd was pressed all the way up to the rope's edges from the back walls. Those in the front were seated so that those in the back could see. Children were given pride of place at the very front of the crowd, all frisking eagerly for Iolaire. Iolaire was frisking for them too. It expected huge amounts of petting.

Caden was honestly impressed by how controlled the crowd was. That might have been aided by the fact that there were Shifters positioned all around the outside edge of the roped off area every five feet, not to mention that there were more Shifters circulating in the crowd and clamping down on any potential criminal activity. Caden had a feeling the ones around the roped off circle were Swarm Shifters, though he couldn't say exactly why. Maybe it was the way they moved in this jittery motion followed by periods of extreme stillness. The ones in the crowd appeared to be Rat and Snake Shifters slithering about. There were no police or Claw.

Valerius had originally objected to this, banging one hand on the arm of his throne. "Marban, I will not have a meet and greet with Iolaire turned into a festival for criminal behavior! Pickpocketing! Mugging! And who knows what else! There needs to be order! Captains Simi and Ngoye can--"

"As you have so graciously pointed out before, King Valerius, I control the Below," Marban had interrupted smoothly. He stroked the front of his monk's robes. "I can assure you that there will not be *one* act of criminality during Caden's visit."

"You can really make that happen?" Caden had asked. He had gone up onto the dais to be a part of this argument.

"Of course, dear boy." Marban smiled so easily it looked as if his mouth was oiled. "Everything will be perfect for you and Rose's special event."

Rose joined them on the dais. Her hands worked nervously together. "When it was going to be a spontaneous event, Grandfather, I didn't worry about things getting rowdy, but now with... ah, with *everything* you've planned and the excitement that Iolaire causes--not to mention the press--things could go pear-shaped."

"You don't think I can control my own people, Granddaughter?" Marban's voice was dangerously reasonable, but Caden could see the mobster's temper underneath. No one in his organization, not even Rose, could question him like this.

"I'm just worried about people in other parts of the city hearing and trying to come down," Rose quickly amended. "They don't respect the Below or the people in it!"

Marban appeared mollified. Caden felt a flare of anger that there had been any threat in Marban's voice to Rose at all. The king of the underworld hadn't truly left that darkness behind no matter that he was on the highest peak in sunshine.

"That is something the Claw can handle. I understand that the lifts and the great staircase have been shut down already," Marban said almost sweetly at Simi.

The Claw Captain, who had been silently watching this exchange, clearly did not like that Marban knew the Claw's activities. "Indeed they have. But people may try to enter the Below through the Gash."

"My people have that handled. Believe me, dozens of Swarm Shifters have been placed near that entrance. They will be shifted, of course. That should keep the others away." Marban spread his hands as if he were offering a generous gift.

"The whole idea of Rose and I doing this was so it would be fun and show that the people in the Below are good and just like everyone else," Caden pointed out. "Do you really think Swarm Shifters guarding the entrances will do that?"

Rose looked unhappy as well at this. "He's right, Grandfather. Just the mention of Swarm Shifters scare people. Do we really want to try to tell people not to be afraid on the one hand while using their supposed scariness with the other?"

Marban tapped his chin, clearly listening to them, which is more than Caden would have thought. "Perhaps Claw there would be more appropriate."

"I can have it arranged right away, King Valerius," Simi said smartly.

"Make it so," Valerius told him.

Simi turned to go, but Marban called out, "No Claw, however, will be inside the Below! That is the one condition that I will not let go!"

Simi looked at Valerius to see if that was all right. After a long moment, Valerius nodded.

The Black Dragon King turned to Marban and pointed a finger directly at the Swarm Shifter's chest. "If anything goes wrong, Marban, this will be on *you*. No one else."

Marban bowed.

But Rose was front and center in this. She was in the center of the roped circle by Marban's side. She seemingly was the only Bee Shifter there, at least if the clothing was any indication of the type of Shifters there. She was dressed in her extreme yellow and black best. Her makeup was more exaggerated than normal. From the way that people were reacting to her--calling her name almost shyly and others asking for her autograph--she was well known and Marban had made it quite clear in his announcement that Iolaire and Rose were good friends.

"Rose looks nervous and unhappy despite the smile she has plastered on her face," Kaila remarked.

"She does not believe that Marban can keep things contained." Valerius grimaced. "I think she is correct. The size of this crowd and its boisterousness are like dry tinder. All it will take is a spark. I hope I do not regret keeping the Claw on the outside."

"I don't know if the Claw makes people here feel safer," Caden said gently.

Valerius' lips thinned. "No, you are likely right. Though Captain Simi has tried to urge the people here to see the Claw as their partners, it has not gone to plan."

"Rose looks like she wants to escape her skin," Kaila continued.

"She doesn't like the spotlight either. Remember, being a Swarm

Shifter has made her isolated as it is. Now she's back in it as my friend, which will get her some more bad attention," Caden explained with a sigh. Marban had really put her in a spot.

Kaila's forehead furrowed. "Bad attention?"

"People will now want to befriend her in the hopes of getting to Caden," Valerius stated flatly.

"She and I were going to do this together before so she knew she'd get some exposure. But this feels different. It's more of an… attraction or something." Caden shivered a little. The Below was cold and he was naked underneath the cloak. His clothes were tucked under Valerius' arm. Shifting would have destroyed them and he loved those jeans.

"People are often quite terrible." Kaila shrugged. "That is why my dolphins are my best friends. They do not like you for any other reasons than they do."

"You are very lucky, Kaila." Valerius put his arm around Caden's shoulders and rubbed them. "Are you all right, Caden?"

"You mean besides the fact that there are thousands of people here waiting to see me? Or that Marban is running the show? Or that I have my usual performance anxiety?" The panic bubbled in his belly again. Always, he feared not being able to shift on command no matter how many times he'd done it, which, in all honesty, wasn't that many.

Iolaire chirruped at him. It was saying everything would be fine

So long as you are in charge, Iolaire, then it will. Just don't let me get carried away, Caden said.

Iolaire lifted its chin proudly while at the same time assuring Caden that he was wonderful too.

Valerius squeezed him and leaned down to whisper in his ear, "Remember the moonlight and the *piercing.*"

Caden let out a bark of laughter that was loud enough that people in the noisy crowd just beyond the stall's hanging carpets that separated them heard him. Caden slammed a hand on his own mouth to silence himself. He then glared at Valerius for making him laugh that loud and hard. Valerius smirked, completely unrepentant.

"Oh! Oh! I think something is happening! Yes, yes, I think it's time!" Kaila jumped up and down on her hoverboard.

There was a crackle and a thumping noise as Marban checked his microphone. "Hello, everyone!"

The crowd roared a hello back.

"Thank you so much for joining us today." Marban gave that monk's smile of benevolence. "We have something very exciting planned for you. The White Dragon Shifter has requested to make an appearance in the Below today!"

There were cries of joy. Caden, though, was *not* joyful. All of this "we" business without mentioning Rose at all! She was just standing there quietly, head down, while Marban took all of the credit. It had nothing to do with him at all. Not to mention, Marban was acting as if Caden had to get *his* permission to appear anywhere in Valerius' city! One glance at Valerius' deepening scowl told Caden that the Black Dragon King was not pleased.

"I'm going out there," Caden said as he prepared to slip through the crowd and into the roped off walkway.

"But he hasn't announced you yet," Kaila pointed out, though she looked as dubious about Marban's speech as the rest of them.

"No, he hasn't. But this isn't about him. And it's about time he got that message," Caden said with a tight smile.

Valerius cupped his face. There was a look of pride as he gazed down at Caden. "Your father fears you don't have the necessary strength to stand up for yourself and others against the most powerful Shifters."

Caden lifted his chin much like Iolaire had earlier. "He's wrong about that."

"I know." Valerius then kissed him. "I cannot wait to see what you do next."

Dazed and yet strengthened by the kiss. Caden staggered out from behind the stall and onto the walkway. He could do this. He would do this. Valerius and Kaila were going to watch from behind the stall. This was his and Rose's show. There would be no one and nothing else to take away from that.

And Caden felt confident.

Even as the too long cloak almost had him tripping and falling on his face. Even as he began to sweat in it. But he couldn't take it off or hoist it up or even adjust the hood so he could see better. He was going to shift while wearing the robe so as to keep his identity a secret for a little while longer. Not to mention that he wasn't going to give Marban that scoop, too. But also, they needed to plan things out for his family. So the cloak and hood stayed on.

But the moment that people started to notice him, the cloak and hood felt completely insufficient. They were going to see him! They were going to know! And what if he couldn't shift?

He heard Marban droning on, but no one was paying attention. Rose's head shot up and she was looking at Caden's ungainly walk towards her. A smile twitched on her lips. The crowd's growing verbal excitement had even Marban stopping speaking as he realized no one cared what he had to say.

Awed chants of "Iolaire! Iolaire!" filled the Below. His Spirit's name echoed all around them. Caden suddenly smiled. All doubt fell away. He strode forward confidently and instead of waiting until he was fully in the circle, Caden shifted.

There were screams of delight and amazement as the White Dragon appeared and the cloak and hood were shredded. Iolaire gracefully kept their wings and tail away from the crowd as they moved into the circle and went directly for Rose. They lowered their head and let out a puff of frost. This was all Iolaire's idea. The frost caused what looked to be a crown to appear over Rose's head. There were gasps. Rose reached up and grasped their head with no fear and kissed their nose.

Caden grinned. *We've got this!*

MIS-JUDGMENT

*V*alerius tugged his hood up as he stepped out from behind the stall and into the crowd to watch Caden, Iolaire and Rose's triumph. Kaila followed after him. She was huffing and fussing with the matching hood and cloak she wore and mourning her hover-board. He'd made her leave it behind.

"This cloak smells musty!" she hissed.

"It's leather. It's meant to smell that way," Valerius said, nettled despite his happiness that things seemed to be going well for Caden and the others. "You did not have to wear one. In fact, I believe I told you that two tall hooded figures--"

"Three! Iolaire was wearing one too!" Kaila corrected him. At least, she remembered not to use Caden's name when they were in the crowd.

He grimaced. "Correct, *three* people in black cloaks and hoods would look suspicious. I recommended that you stay behind the stall."

"But I couldn't see!" Kaila complained. "And I came here to see things! So here I am!"

"I thought you came here to support Iolaire and Rose." Valerius gave her a reproachful look as she shifted under her hood and cloak like a person wearing a very bad disguise. Luckily, all eyes were on Iolaire and Rose at that moment.

He noted the awe-filled gazes in the people's eyes. Not just awe-filled but almost *giddy* looks that people were giving Iolaire. The children who were in the front row--and were being lined up expertly by Rose to pet Iolaire--were blissed out with delight.

I do not think that people look at us that way, Raziel, Valerius said to his Spirit, half in jest and half in... well, he wasn't sure what.

No, but it is not our role to be beloved, his Spirit surprisingly answered. *Let them love Iolaire. Let them fear us.*

And Valerius saw the logic in this. Iolaire and Caden could be--actually perhaps already *were*--the silk glove over his and Raziel's steel fist. While it would be beneath his and Raziel's dignity to let a child ride his tail--which was happening right now with Iolaire--it was Caden and Iolaire's joy to do so. And it only added to their mystique which was, again, so very different from his and Raziel's. Raziel curled in a ball and let its eyelids slowly close as it dreamed of Iolaire.

"Do your people adore you and Lana like that, Kaila?" Valerius was honestly curious. The two of them had not ever let their conversations stray beyond what needed to be said. Kaila, honestly, exhausted and irritated him with her boundless energy and humming bird-like thoughts.

Kaila cocked her head to the side, considering this, which also caused her hood to sag. "The dolphins do."

"I meant your human and Shifter subjects," Valerius said dryly.

"Oh, I don't know. I don't think so. They are happy to see me as I make sure their nets are full of fish but they are not..." Kaila paused as she tried to sum up the emotion in the Below, "drunk with happiness like this. Here it is as if Iolaire is the sun and they are all flowers starved for light."

Considering that the Below was indeed starved for sunlight it was an apt description. Valerius frowned as he took in the faces around him. Many looked haggard, cheeks hollowed out and dark circles under their eyes. People had clearly dressed in their very best but the clothing was still a little ragged. The world in which he had been born into had always had the haves and the have nots. In fact, there were far more have nots than haves back then. In many ways that hadn't changed.

As he continued to look around, Valerius felt a sense of dissatisfaction. He had never been the type of ruler who had pledged to end inequality. He did not believe that was possible. He was not the type of ruler to pander to the poor either, promising them things he could never deliver. He didn't pander to the rich either. He ignored everyone. But what he saw here was troubling. This was *his* main city. His castle was perched high above these people perhaps so far above them that he hadn't *seen* them or the desperate poverty and want that was before him now.

"Look at all the little fish wary of the big fish! Just waiting to be eaten," Kaila said with a shake of her head.

It took him a moment to understand what she meant. Her "big fish" were the Swarm, Rat and Snake Shifters who ran the gangs while the "little fish" was evidently everyone else.

Marban had his "big fish" patrolling the "little fish" to make sure there was no crime or violence to ruin the show. Considering all the cameras here filming not only Iolaire, but panning across the crowd, Valerius understood on some level why. Anyone misbehaving who was from the Below would be used as an example of *every* person from the Below. In fact, a reporter was breathlessly saying something akin to that to her colleague.

"I have to admit, Roger, that I haven't ever been in the Below other than during my time as a local reporter doing crime stories," the reed-thin peroxide blond said to a smiling man in a well-cut suit.

"I hear you, Linda!" Roger agreed with her over brightly. "I have to say that things down here are hopping! I haven't seen so many smiles since... well, since Iolaire made its appearance in Dragon Strike Square."

Linda nodded so loosely that Valerius thought that she might have strings controlling that movement. "Indeed! And wasn't that a lovely time! Do you think now that Iolaire has made an appearance in the

Below and Mid that we can expect the ninth Dragon Shifter to show up on every level?"

Roger laughed avuncularly. "Well, we already know Iolaire is spending quite a bit of time in High Reach meeting its brethren. But we can always hope!"

"Oh, look! There seems to be some sort of commotion over there! With that young boy and one of the, ah, uhm, Snake Shifters, I think?" Linda gestured towards where a bald man with a snake tattooed around his throat like a noose had clamped a hand down on the back of a boy's neck.

The boy didn't look to be more than thirteen to Valerius. He scowled as he watched the Snake Shifter lift the boy up to a standing position, he'd been sitting, and spin him around. His eyes were narrowed and a decidedly nasty look was on his face. It was then that the Snake Shifter realized that one of the cameras was pointed towards him. He suddenly smiled--smiles did not seem to come naturally to him--and wrapped a seemingly friendly arm around the boy whom he pressed close against his side. He waved as if he were *excited* to be on television.

"I guess it wasn't what I thought. Appears that they know one another," Linda burbled and the two of them went back to discussing just how clean the Below was.

Valerius watched as the Snake Shifter, now no longer on television, turned the friendly hug into a headlock and dragged the boy through the crowd towards the back wall. Valerius started moving after them. Kaila followed him.

"Where are we going?" she asked avidly.

"To see what Marban thinks justice looks like," Valerius answered her.

He might have allowed bad things to happen in the Below when he wasn't looking, but he wasn't going to let something occur right in front of his eyes. He took one glance back at Iolaire. There were over a dozen children riding Iolaire's tail now and even more climbing onto its back. Iolaire was making it snow.

Rose was involved in a raucous snowball fight. Valerius smirked when a snowball hit Marban's bald pate. Rose put her hands up to her mouth to keep the laughter in as the snow and ice slid down his face. Valerius paused, wary that Marban would get angry at the affront and ruin everything, but the wily Swarm Shifter suddenly ducked down like a man half his age to form a snowball of his own that he threw at Rose. Soon, Marban was tossing and dodging snowballs. Satisfied that everything and everyone here was all right, he turned back to the boy with the Snake Shifter.

He and Kaila glided through the crowd. People made way even in the densely packed space. They didn't know who he or Kaila were, but everyone sensed not to get in their way. One man went so far as to suck his stomach in to give Valerius another inch of space. Kaila poked him in the tummy causing the man to grunt and let the air out. She chuckled as they passed.

"Kaila, we are keeping a low profile. The cloaks and hoods, remember?" Valerius hissed at her.

"Oh, you're no fun!" She sighed but stopped herself from touching any other pedestrian.

Valerius watched as the Snake Shifter took the boy through a door guarded by two Rat Shifters. The Rat Shifters immediately sidled back into place, blocking the door completely even though neither of them were more than five feet tall and skinny as rails.

Few people were scared of Rat Shifters. In Wally's former life, Valerius remembered that he had made his mark in the underworld by being smart and using force as the last option. He'd also organized the Rat Shifters into large groups that bound together. There was nothing quite as horrifying as hundreds of rats swarming. But Marban hadn't kept Wally's way of running the Rat Shifters. Or maybe with the crowds there simply weren't enough Shifters to keep more than two Rats together.

The two Rat Shifters noticed Valerius and Kaila approaching--and how could they not both of them towering over much of the crowd, not to mention the hoods and cloaks?--and immediately their noses were twitching. Valerius could almost imagine the whiskers that would be there in their rat forms.

Valerius stopped about two feet from the Rat Shifters. He loomed above them. He doubted they could see his face clearly even this close up as the shadows were much deeper here away from the stage.

"Get lost, long legs!" the Rat Shifter to the right said with a stab of one pudgy finger towards Valerius' stomach. He would have had to lift his hand higher to aim at Valerius' chest.

"Long legs? Oh, that's a great nickname! Now do me! Do me!" Kaila clapped.

The two Rat Shifters looked at one another as if Kaila had lost her mind. Valerius did not blame them. He often thought the same.

The Rat Shifter to the left growled at her, "How about I call you 'dead meat', because that's what you're going to be if you don't beat it!"

"That's not very nice. I was hoping for a nickname, not an insult!" Kaila fumed.

"What's in there?" Valerius asked.

"Nothing you need to know about, long legs!" the right Rat Shifter spit.

Valerius envisioned ripping back the hood and leaning down right into those pugnacious faces and watching as their looks of defiance became ones of fear. But he couldn't do that because news that he was there would spread. It would likely cause a riot, not because people would be running towards him--asking for pets or tail rides, thank goodness!--but rather racing *away* in terror. The last time he was here, he'd killed people after all. So relying on who he was wasn't going to work.

"I'm curious about the boy the Snake Shifter brought in there," Valerius said.

The two Rat Shifters looked at each other like two ugly book ends and chortled.

"Ah, little Stevie will finally get what's coming to him!" The Rat Shifter on his right held his stomach as he let out a deep belly laugh.

"What is Stevie's supposed crime? He looks all of thirteen," Valerius said.

"Stevie's been a thief since he came out of his mama's womb and stole her life!" The Rat Shifter on the left found that little line hysterical.

Valerius' hands fisted at his sides. "And he was caught stealing now?"

"Pickpocketing! I'm sure George found him trying to lift a wallet or two." The Rat Shifter on the right shrugged.

"He's violated Marban's rules. He's bound to get the Chop!"

More chortling.

"What do you mean 'the Chop'?" Kaila was frowning at them. Valerius could hear it in her voice but couldn't see her face.

"None of your business, dead meat." The Rat Shifter on the right found that even funnier than anything they'd said so far.

But Valerius didn't imagine anything named "the Chop" could be good. He thought of how thieves in certain cultures had their hands chopped off. Could that be what was to be Stevie's fate?

"Marban wants a tween to be punished severely for pickpocketing even if he doesn't have enough food to eat or shelter to keep himself warm and dry?" Valerius heard the outrage in his voice.

The Rat Shifter on the left snarled, "Marban does what he can for those who can pull their weight and follow the rules. If you want to blame someone, blame fate."

"Blame the President of the United States! Blame King Valerius!" The Rat Shifter on the right gave him a narrow eyed glance.

"You blame Valerius for this? For the evil *you* do? For the harming of a child?" Kaila growled. "If not for Valerius, the Shifters would be on human dissection tables or in their jails or buried six feet under! If not for Valerius, Illarion would have you all in his work camps or Mei would be putting your little rat brains in her mechanical men! Valerius makes it possible for you to live a good life and do the right thing! If you choose not to... well, that is your choice!"

As she made this impassioned defense of him, she put her hands on her hips which caused the cloak to flare out and reveal a snippet of her island outfit. The Rat Shifters' beady eyes lit up. They thought they saw a mark. And that gave Valerius an idea. He needed to get past the Rat Shifters and into that room *without* picking them up like the sacks of garbage they were and throwing them, which would cause a commotion. If Kaila lured them away then his problem would be solved

"Dear, your defense of Valerius is quite vociferous, but I think you're not going to convert others. These two have their ideas pretty set," Valerius said.

"Hell, yeah!" The left Rat Shifter pounded one fist into the palm of his open hand. "If I had Valerius here I'd show him what's what."

"Indeed, you look quite capable of taking down the largest Dragon Shifter in the world," Valerius replied dryly. If Raziel hadn't been asleep, Valerius could only imagine what his Spirit would say to the Rat Shifter's boasts.

"Don't we though!" The two Rat Shifters elbowed each other.

"Quite. Dear," he said to Kaila, "these gentlemen seem very keen connoisseurs of your clothes. I think they would appreciate your jewelry even more. Perhaps you could show it to them."

Kaila's voice was filled with disgust, "My jewelry? But they're Raaaa--"

"I think they would appreciate it. Over there." Valerius pointed to a rather dimly lit corner. "Where it would be safe to show them. Away from other prying eyes that wouldn't be as *noble* as these two."

Valerius hoped he wasn't laying on it too thick but these two didn't look like their brain pans were too large. He only hoped that Kaila got his intentions. Kaila stared at him blankly. Maybe he could just tell the two bastards that he'd give them "dear's" jewelry if they stepped away quietly. But he tried with Kaila one last time.

"Take them *over there*, dear," Valerius emphasized the location.

Kaila followed his repeated gesture. Finally, knowledge bloomed on her face. "Oh! Yes! Let me show you!" Kaila turned towards the Rat Shifters and exposed the bands of bracelets set with precious jewels that went up and down her forearms. "Aren't they lovely? You can take a closer look over there."

"Well..." The right Rat turned to the left one, their bushy brown eyebrows communicated that this was too rich an opportunity to pass up. "You won't be coming with us, long legs?"

"No." Valerius did not indicate what he was going to do. They likely guessed he was going inside, but the jewelry was too much of an enticement to turn down. Little did they know that Kaila could handle them with both hands tied behind her back.

"Come along, gentlemen. I can't wait to show you everything," Kaila grinned.

The three of them went off together, and immediately, Valerius went for the door. It was locked. He noticed there was a sensor pad to the side. He growled. But then his hearing caught a sharp yelp from a teenager's throat. Valerius immediately thrust through the door. The door shattered into toothpick-sized shards and he raced inside.

The room itself was not large, about twenty by twenty feet square. It was cut out of the living rock, but there were computer monitors attached to every wall and bright fluorescent lights made the room practically glow. Valerius blinked and lifted an arm to shield his eyes even with the hood.

There were wild shouts and he felt a thick, hard body slam into him. He braced himself and skidded only a foot or so along the floor before he was an immovable wall. His vision cleared and he realized he was being tackled--or attempted to be--by a Bear Shifter. For a Shifter, the bear was large and burly, but Valerius was something else altogether.

Fists started flying towards him, but he easily blocked ninety percent of them. The ones that made it through felt like light taps, which for normal people or even Shifters, would have laid them out. It just made him angry though Raziel didn't even stir in its snooze.

"Enough," Valerius said and struck the Bear Shifter once with the flat of his hand.

He kept the blow light, but the man keeled over like a tree felled in the woods and landed on the floor with a thump. Then he turned to the other people in the room. There was only the Snake Shifter called George and the pickpocket, Stevie. But the activities that he saw them in were not what he thought.

George was seated at a desk, watching the monitors. Stevie was standing there with a mop and bucket. George had something in his hand. It was a rubberband. He was firing rubberbands at Stevie as the young man worked.

"I thought that Stevie was getting the Chop," Valerius found himself saying.

"Who are you?" Stevie's voice was high and tight. "Is Burry dead?"

Burry must be the Bear Shifter who was unconscious in a pile on the floor.

Instead of being the savior, Valerius realized how he must have looked: cloaked, hooded and huge, having laid out their Bear Shifter and demanding to know why Stevie *wasn't* getting the Chop.

This is going all wrong.

"Burry is fine. He just should--"

Kaila danced into the room. She was laughing and spinning. "Those Rat Shifters have learned their lesson about trying to steal jewelry from--"

"You hurt Ralphie and Dickie?" Stevie cried.

Kaila stopped dancing. Now they were two hooded and cloaked figures who had taken out their compatriots.

Things are really going badly.

"Isn't this the boy who was going to have his hands chopped off or something?" Kaila pointed to Stevie.

"My--my hands cut off?" Stevie squeaked.

"What does 'the chop' mean?" Valerius demanded of George.

"It means that his freedom is limited until he makes amends! Jesus, man, what do you think? That I would hurt a kid?" George looked outraged.

Valerius' shoulders slumped. Marban was better than most Dragon Shifters would have been. He had misjudged the man. Well, maybe he wouldn't go that far. He turned to Kaila with a kind of dread. "Please tell me that you didn't kill those Rat Shifters."

"What? No! They were sort of cute actually. I said I'd meet them for drinks later after they woke up," Kaila said brightly.

"Oh, good." Valerius smiled and turned back to George. That was when he happened to see the image on the monitors over George's shoulder and he tensed.

Streaming down the steps, having somehow gotten through the Claw up above and Marban's Shifters down below, were members of the Faith in their white flowing robes.

His mind went to the fact that the crowd here was huge.

An explosion here would definitely cause many deaths.

And perhaps an opportunity for people to join with Spirits.

THE SCENT OF DANGER

The Below extravaganza was going better than expected. Caden grinned down at Rose who was helping another little girl up onto his and Iolaire's back. The people already perched there leaned down to grasp the girl's hands and pulled her up to join them.

Iolaire flapped their wings--carefully and just once--and the snow that had settled on the ground of the Below flew up into the air again and came sparkling down. Caden saw a father lift up his son so that he could get some of it on his tongue. The boy giggled and clasped his father's neck with two chubby arms in delight.

Everywhere there were faces full of joy and delight. Even the Shifters assigned to monitor the event were grinning or, at least, not looking as grim as usual. There was a lightness to the air like champagne where happiness bubbled up in steady streams.

This was what he, Rose and Iolaire had planned for this event, even before Marban got "involved". The fact that it was still going so well even with Marban's *additions* was gratifying. He almost felt like he could breathe. The event was going to go off without a hitch!

"Marban," a female reporter with closely cropped black hair said as she sidled up to the crime boss. Marban, of course, looked anything *like* a crime boss with his paunch and grandfather's wrinkled face. "How did this event come about?"

Caden fought not to roll his eyes. She was asking the *wrong* person.

"Well, I had the honor of meeting Iolaire that terrible first day they joined with their human partner," Marban said, showing just the right amount of sadness at the remembered events. Caden tensed. Was Marban going to trash Valerius?

"Indeed." The reporter scented a scoop. Clearly, she hadn't thought that Marban would bring up the tragedy. "What explanation did Iolaire give for its battle with Raziel?"

It wasn't a battle! It was a scuffle. Where I ran away and got very lucky!

Iolaire twittered softly at the thought of fighting with Raziel and those who had died.

Marban put his hands together in front of him as if in prayer. "It was truly a tragedy, Marta."

He knows the reporter's name? Oh, man, Marban is always working it!

The reporter, Marta, lit up and immediately jumped in with the obvious, which had Caden wincing, "Do you blame King Valerius? After all, it was *his* actions in chasing Iolaire here that--"

Marban continued on as if she hadn't spoken, "... based upon a terrible misunderstanding and King Valerius' desire to protect the people. You see, King Valerius and Raziel, in the heat of the moment, made the understandable connection that Iolaire was somehow involved with the bombing."

"Not to mention finding another Dragon in their territory, unannounced and uninvited." Marta's tone was dry.

Marban nodded, consenting to this as well. "It was a shock. A shock all around. And it led to a terrible accident."

The reporter blinked as if she couldn't possibly have heard Marban right. "I believe that's the talking points from High Reach. I didn't expect them from you, Marban."

For one moment--though Caden didn't think the reporter or even most of the viewers caught it--Marban's expression became sly as he answered her, "I have--and always will--speak truth to power."

Like you have no power, Marban?!

"But, in this case, the truth is what has come from High Reach," Marban continued with an almost helpless shrug. "And I will state it far and wide."

It was now the reporter's turn to look sly. "I heard that you have been named to a new Shifter Council that King Valerius is setting up. And that this appointment was made *right after* Iolaire's appearance."

Oh, boy. So yeah, uhm, that looks bad,

"Do you really think that King Valerius would create a Shifter Council on a whim and put me on it, Marta?" Marban was tutting and shaking his head. "The Shifter Council has been planned for some time. That you are only now finding out about it is... well, getting insider information out of High Reach is always difficult."

Marta's expression hardened slightly. "So you're saying that your appointment to this Council, Iolaire's appearance and the deaths of over a dozen people in the Below are *not* connected?"

Marban's smile seemed to grow. "What I am saying is simply this: that a Shifter Council, where a citizen from the Below is prominently featured, can *never* be a detriment to the Below, Marta."

Marta opened her mouth to ask more questions, but two Snake Shifters were suddenly at her side, leading her away from Marban even as she protested.

"Wait! I have more questions--"

"Others have to get their time in too with Marban," one of the Snake Shifters hissed into the shell of her ear.

She looked affronted and then paled when she caught sight of the man's serpentine smile.

"Thank you, Marta! Always good to see you!" Marban waved at her and Caden had a feeling she would not be welcomed for any further interviews.

She's smart though. She connected some dots. But Marban is also right. The Shifter Council and his closeness with Valerius will only help the people here, Caden thought. *I wonder where Valerius is.*

He glanced back towards the stalls where he had left Valerius and Kaila, but he saw no signs of their hooded heads. He hoped that Kaila hadn't decided to use her hoverboard or do something else that would attract attention. Kaila was not discrete. He supposed most Dragons weren't.

Caden felt a light touch on their shoulder. He looked down and saw Marban standing there, one hand on Iolaire's shimmering white scales. The wily old Swarm Shifter was looking all around him. Marban had a soft smile on his lips that was not one that Caden had ever seen there before. Certainly not one he'd used on camera. He thought it might be an actual *genuine* smile. Marban glanced up at him. Their gazes met. The Swarm Shifter smiled more broadly and nodded his head as if to say, "This is good. Better than good. And I did not expect it."

Of course, that was when things went sideways.

Marban lifted his right hand to his right ear where there was a bluetooth device. The words were too low for Caden to hear over the roar of the crowd, but he saw Marban's expression change from one of happiness to alarm to anger then a blank mask replaced them all.

What's happened? What's wrong?

But Marban couldn't hear him. Only Iolaire realized his alarm. Again, Caden searched for Valerius, but he didn't sense Raziel or Valerius' minds at that moment, so he couldn't even reach out to them to talk to Marban on his behalf. This was the biggest downside of being in their Dragon form. They couldn't talk to anybody really.

Damnit! What's happening?

Marban moved quickly to Rose's side. He was all smiles again, but those smiles were plastic and strained. They were not genuine. But the cameras would show nothing wrong. The crowd would just see the same fond grandfatherly figure that had always been there and always would be.

But Caden knew better and anxiety had him almost flickering their long tail too fast. Iolaire took over and stopped the children from being thrown end over end. Instead, they just let out delighted laughs as the tail moved *a little* faster than it had before, more like an adult ride than a kiddie one. His focus though was on Marban and Rose.

What is wrong?

Marban was pulling Rose away from the children so they could talk privately, or as privately as they could in the middle of a crowd with cameras rolling. Rose frowned and tried to gently shake him off, but Marban was not letting go. There was a plaintive cry from the children on his tail. Evidently, both he and Iolaire were now distracted and had stopped moving their tail altogether. Iolaire quickly restarted the steady swaying while they both looked back at Marban and Rose.

The two of them were scanning the crowd. Not those near to them, but farther back, towards the Stairs. Rose suddenly jerked her hand towards the landing. It was then that Caden caught sight of the white robed figures. His heart was in Iolaire's long throat.

The Faith!

Before when he had seen the Faith, the most Caden would have felt about them was annoyance and a bit of embarrassment. They had always just seemed like a group of too earnest people who Caden secretly believed wanted to be Shifters with all the benefits that brought. It was like the poor worshiping the rich for all the benefits that money brought, but claiming they didn't want any wealth for themselves. Though his mother was quick to assure him--and anyone who asked--that wasn't the case with her and, sometimes, he believed her. But now seeing the Faith had a cold chill running down his spine.

Is there another bomb set someplace? This would be the perfect event to "make" some more Shifters, Caden realized with a sickening lurch.

Iolaire twittered uneasily.

Do you sense anything, Iolaire? Can you, uhm, sense bombs? Like maybe smell them? Caden asked, knowing that was hugely unlikely.

Iolaire responded in the negative. Not at this distance at least. But maybe if it was nearer they could. Yet between them and the filing line of Faith that were flowing into the Below, there were thousands of people. How could they get close enough to them without crushing people?

His gaze swept the crowd, looking for Valerius for a third time, but the cloaked and hooded figure of the massive Black Dragon King was not anywhere to be seen. He half expected to see Kaila dancing out into the crowd regardless of the Faith. But she was not there either.

Where are they?

But then he realized that even if he could find them, Valerius and Kaila acting against the Faith would be a bad thing. Unless it was done really carefully.

Caden looked down and saw Marban speaking furiously over his bluetooth device. He still had a smile plastered on his face, but it fit tight across his tense features. Through the roar of the crowd, Caden heard the words, "Faith", "round up", "block off", "sniffer" and "now, absolutely now!"

Rose was trying to interact with the kids with that bright and sunny expression from before but her eyes were tracking the crowd worriedly. She glanced up at him and mouthed, "Faith." He gave a brief nod to show he understood.

Once more his gaze slid towards the crowd. He saw Shifters moving through the people towards the Stairs, but there were too many people in their way. Some of the Shifters were totally blocked from moving forward. They started to shove, but there simply wasn't room for the people to go. They were not going to be in time to stop the white robed figures of the Faith from fanning out into the crowd.

What if one of them has a bomb? Caden thought again. He remembered the explosion and a flash of white and Iolaire's voice. There had been no pain, but his heart beat faster and his breathing increased. *They have to be stopped.*

He looked down at Marban and the Swarm Shifter caught his eye. He knew in that instant that Marban understood that his people were not going to get to the Faith in time, not in their human forms anyways. But swarms of rats, snakes and insects appearing in the middle of the crowd would cause a huge panic. People could be injured, or even killed, as they raced for the exits and some ended up getting trampled or crushed against walls. The news people would record it all and what had been a wonderful moment for the Below would become yet another tragedy. Marban knew this too and he looked almost defeated at that moment.

It was then that Iolaire sent him an image of them hovering over the crowd in front of the Faith. There was plenty of room in the air.

Yes! Perfect, Iolaire! Let's do it!

Caden had Iolaire shake their head violently at Marban to indicate he shouldn't give the command to shift. Not yet anyways. Then it was with incredibly gentleness that Iolaire sent the children sliding off of its tail and back, only to be caught by surprised parents. Iolaire flapped their wings then. People put hands up to block their eyes as gusts of wind whipped up snow and dirt from the ground. Soon they were hovering ten feet above the ground then twenty. There were ooohhhhs and ahhhhhs from everyone. They had no idea why he and Iolaire were doing this other than to show off some of their flying.

Iolaire glided towards the platform at the bottom of the Stairs where the Faith were gathering and about to stream out into the crowd itself. Most everyone was gazing up at Iolaire in awe. Caden looked for those who *weren't*. He figured if he was carrying a bomb, he'd be more intent on that then even watching a Dragon hovering over him. But the wind from Iolaire's wings was flattening the hoods against the members' heads and it was hard to tell who wasn't looking because of guilt and who wasn't because it was impossible to do so.

We can't stay up here, Iolaire! He told his Spirit. *We need to get down there! We need to block them!*

Iolaire started to lower them to the ground. It wanted to be between the crowd and the Faith. This would be close enough to see if it detected any chemicals that might mean there was a bomb on one or more of the Faith.

What if they detonate the bomb now?

Caden's gaze skittered over the white robed figures. He figured if they did that that they would use their massive body and wings to block the blast from reaching the majority of the crowd. People were, thankfully, scattering as Iolaire made this unexpected landing. They settled down in the half-moon space.

Be big. Be bad, Iolaire. We need to impress them. Pretend you're Raziel! Caden told the Spirit.

Iolaire twittered that they only needed to be themselves, but the

White Dragon Spirit did have them "puff" up so they looked even bigger than they were. They sat up on their haunches. Their wings were spread wide. And then Iolaire breathed on the steps between the Below and the Faith until they were covered in a sheet of ice. No one was easily getting down those without falling on their asses.

Good idea, Iolaire!

The crowd had gone very quiet. News crews who had been filming the scene from the far edges of the Below now had a perfect view of this confrontation up close and personal.

He heard a male reporter breathlessly saying, "Iolaire has turned the steps to ice. One would almost say that it is trying to keep the Faith out of the Below. But why?"

Why indeed? No one is going to easily believe that the Faith could be behind these bombings! Caden thought with a touch of dismay.

A woman, the leader of his mother's sect, came forward with a beatific smile on her face. She seemed completely unaware of the possibility that the reporter had voiced that they were keeping the Faith away from everyone else as best he could. The leader--he thought her name was Joanna--stopped about two-feet from the iced steps and raised her arms. This caused the Faith to break out into a soft and moving melody that seemed to float up in glorious waves to the ceiling. Caden only winced when he listened to the lyrics.

"Oh, White Dragon. Oh, Ninth Dragon. Oh, Ice King or Queen. We call to thee for guidance and morality--"

Who thought up those lyrics, Iolaire? Caden groaned.

But he quickly shook off any interest in the song and looked at the people. Those damned hoods were blocking faces. Everyone was singing in unison, making these arm movements in a coordinated effort that reminded him of a combination of Walk Like An Egyptian video and Irish dance. It was more polished than their usual stuff, likely because they knew they were going to be on television.

Iolaire, we've got to make sure that none of these people have any explosives on them! Caden reminded his Spirit.

Iolaire twittered its understanding. Immediately, it lowered their head to the leader. Her smile widened as Iolaire pressed their snout to her chest and breathed in. She clasped their head in an awkward embrace, singing loudly of her joy.

Nothing there. God, though, she wears too much perfume! Lilacs!

Iolaire disengaged them from her embrace and went to the next person at the end of the line to their left. That person immediately stepped forward and embraced Iolaire just as the leader had. Again, no scent of chemicals.

Does C4 smell like anything? Caden wondered.

And even if it did, would they recognize its scent? Would they sniff every single person and miss the obvious? But Iolaire seemed confident they'd discover the person if there was a person to be found.

Another reporter had joined the first and he heard them saying over the continued singing, "Aww, Iolaire is letting the Faith hug it!"

The first reporter chuckled, "Yes. Is Iolaire sniffing them?"

"It might be! Maybe that's its way of greeting?" the second replied.

"Let's hope it isn't smelling them for tastiness!" the first reporter chortled.

Iolaire was sniffing the fifth person. Caden kept looking down the line of Faith. Was anyone reacting differently? Tense at their approach? Sidling away? Trying to hide something?

While quite a few of the Faith were eagerly looking down the line towards them, waiting for their chance to embrace him and Iolaire, there were just as many not looking. Some had their eyes closed as they sang their hearts out. Others appeared to just be murmuring. Others had their faces hidden.

Which one of you is guilty? Caden wondered. *Is one of you guilty?*

He thought he saw one of the people about five down twitch when they moved their head to the next person. He fixed one of their blue eyes on this person. They had their hood pulled down and were definitely shifting nervously.

Iolaire, skip the rest of these people! Go to them! They are looking suspicious!

His Spirit complied and bypassed the next person who nearly toppled over as they thought his and Iolaire's snout would have been there to catch them. Instead, they glared down at the figure who suspiciously kept their hood pulled down almost to their chin. Their blue eyes narrowed! This person was *definitely* acting suspiciously. They loomed over the hooded figure.

I won't let you hurt anyone! Caden hissed.

Then they leaned in and the hooded member of the Faith slowly put their arms around his snout. They drew in a deep breath and...

Mom?!

There was no scent of C4 or any other explosive, just his mother's clean scent of sandalwood and cinnamon. She hugged him fiercely.

"Iolaire," she whispered, but he heard his own name somehow in the name of his Spirit.

Mom...

This was the first time that his mother had seen Iolaire up close, let alone touched them. They closed their eyes and purred. He knew they should pull back and not treat her any differently than the rest of the Faith, but he couldn't quite do it. And Iolaire was *loving* being so close to her, too.

You think of her as Mom too? Oh, man, she's going to love that! She's also going to think she's not worthy of that but I can't wait to tell her.

His mother saved them both by drawing back. Her hands drifted over their snout. He could see her face now. Tears were streaming down her cheeks, but she was smiling broadly.

It was in this moment of hesitation, gazing at her lovingly, that Caden and Iolaire caught a whiff of a plasticky, acrid scent. A scent he knew did not belong. A scent Iolaire knew to mean danger.

It was a member of the Faith with a bomb.

And they were standing right next to his mother.

BOMB BELIEVER

Earlier...

*V*alerius pushed past George to look at the video feeds. The Snake Shifter let out a "Hey, who do you think you are?" but then Valerius swept back his hood from his head, and George gasped, "You?! King Valerius?!"

"You're quite observant. Let's see if you can do me!" Kaila shook back her hood.

But all George said was, "You're quite pretty."

"Yes." Kaila tossed her hair back. "Yes, I am. But you don't know who I am."

"You're, uhm, an actress or something?" George cocked his head to the side.

"He doesn't get out much. Or watch TV or the internet," Stevie burst out. "That's Queen Kaila, you idiot! She's another Dragon Shifter. The aquamarine one called Lana."

"Oh!" George's eyes grew large though Valerius was pretty sure that the Snake Shifter didn't know Lana and Kaila from any of the other Dragon Shifters. "That still doesn't explain what you two are doing busting in here!"

"They thought you were torturing me!" Stevie cackled. "I was being rescued by Dragons!"

George stuck a finger in Stevie's face who pushed it away. "You are a reprobate who needs to get back to mopping!"

"All of you, *quiet!*" Valerius growled.

As they had bickered, he had been using the video equipment to focus on the Faith. His gaze flickered over the dozens of white robed figures looking for... what? Guilt on their faces? A bomb strapped to their bodies? Maybe a little bit of both.

"What are you looking at?" George asked.

"The Faith," Valerius growled and spun around to the Snake Shifter. He pointed at the white robed figures. "How did *they* get down here? Marban specifically knew they were not to be let in."

George's mouth opened and shut. Stevie answered for him, "It's impossible to keep them out."

"What do you mean?" Kaila asked.

"Even if you keep the ones wearing white out, there are countless people who aren't wearing the robes," Stevie pointed out. "There were probably people in security who were Faith and let them in."

George gave an uncomfortable shrug. "Faith is above even Marban. You know how they look at Swarm Shifters. Self-hatred is a sad thing."

Valerius gritted his teeth and went back to scanning the video feeds. Kaila came up beside him. She studied the video feeds with him, biting her lower lip, as she too looked for some kind of evidence that one of these Faith members--or more--were up to no good.

"Why are you worried about the Faith? I mean other than the bad songs and stuff." Stevie shuddered at the memory of their songs.

Valerius ignored the boy. Even if he had the time, he had no inclination to scare a child about the Faith. Maybe they were wrong and the Faith wasn't behind the bombings or maybe only *some* of them were. He doubted a boy like Stevie would keep his mouth shut and it would cause a panic.

"We'll never get there from here," Kaila remarked as she took over one of the cameras and panned it over the now, much more packed area around the Stairs than even when they had made their way over. "Not without causing a commotion."

"And we do not want that," Valerius murmured.

Valerius panned one of the cameras to the news crews that were clustered around the Stairs as that gave them the best view of everything happening to prove his point. It wouldn't just be the people in the Below who would see him and Kaila "attacking" the Faith but people all over the world.

There was a hiss and spitting sound before Marban's voice came over the radio, "Attention, Security, you are to *stop* the Faith and turn them back from the Below. Do you hear me? Stop the Faith! Be aware that they may have explosives."

George and Stevie looked at Valerius and Kaila with open mouths.

"E-explosives?" Stevie squeaked. "Is the Faith behind the bombings?"

"We need to get to them. Fast! How can we do this?" Valerius demanded to know.

"There are back passageways. We can take you," George said as he stood up stiff-legged from his rolling chair. He looked a bit in shock. Was he a member of the Faith? Like Stevie had said, anyone could be a believer. They didn't have to wear white and sing bad songs.

This was a mistake. Creating any sort of planned event where thousands of people would gather...

"Take us. Now," Valerius said.

"I'll come too! I know the way better than George!" Stevie offered, just as eager to be in on the action as to leave his mopping duties.

"No, you will not, child," Kaila said as she thrust the mop handle back into the boy's hands.

"Aw, man! Come on! I can get you there faster!" Stevie whined and began to pout.

"You stay here and monitor the radio, Stevie," George told the boy, which immediately had Stevie brightening. "And you radio me any shortcuts that you know."

"Yeah! Awesome! I can do that!" The boy grabbed George's chair and scooted over to the desk where he put on the headset. "Oh, people are having problems getting over there, George!"

"Yeah, I bet, Stevie," George answered grimly.

George went to a cabinet and grabbed a gun from inside of it. He slipped it into the back of his pants. He then stuck a bluetooth device in his right ear. He didn't head towards the door back out into the market area of the Below but instead went to a bank of shelves. He reached between two books and the shelf slid to the side revealing a stone staircase that led up into the bare rock.

"Keep us in the loop, Stevie!" George called back over his shoulder.

"Will do!" The boy made a salute with two fingers.

Valerius wasn't sure if he felt comforted by having a child as their backup but it was as it was. He took the stairs two at a time after George with Kaila on his heels. The staircase was so narrow that he had to almost turn sideways at times to get through. It was lit only by yellow utility lamps that cast a dirty, ugly light over the stone. The air smelled of damp stone and garbage rotting in corners.

"Ugh! What has died in here?" Kaila hissed from behind him. She was used to salt-tinged breezes and the clean scent of coconut. That was not the case here.

George had led them to a T-intersection. Valerius' sense of direction told him that the Stairs should be to their right, but George was hesitating.

"What's wrong? Shouldn't we go to the right?" Valerius asked him.

"One of these tunnels has collapsed," George answered. "I'm not sure if it is this one or the level above this one."

"Should we have brought the boy?" Kaila's right eyebrow rose.

"Contact Stevie if you do not know!" Valerius cried, feeling time ticking down.

George pressed a finger against the bluetooth device in his ear. Even before he had a chance to say anything, even Valerius could hear Stevie's voice rising over the device, "George! George! Iolaire flew over to the Stairs!"

What? Valerius' eyes widened in alarm.

"Iolaire must have seen them coming in," Kaila guessed. "Well, if one of them has a bomb on them, Iolaire will deal with it."

"How? By cuddling them?" Valerius hissed. He knew that was unfair. Iolaire was, of course, capable of violence. Every dragon was. But both Iolaire and Caden were *not* killers and violence of any kind was not natural to them.

"Bah! Iolaire is no lightweight! They will take action to help others," Kaila said with a dismissive wave of her hand.

"I do not want them to have to do anything like that!" Valerius hissed.

Kaila's eyebrows rose. "Oh, well, I see."

He wondered what she did see. He leaned in towards George menacingly. "Find out which way."

George gave a jerky nod and cut off Stevie's excited-panicked patter, "Stevie! Stevie! Chill! King Valerius needs to know if its Level 4a or 4b that's blocked."

"Oh! Yeah, it's like both, dude! Didn't you know that?" Stevie asked. "Where have you been that you--"

"Stevie!" George hissed with a scared glance at Valerius. "How do I get them to the Stairs?"

"Easy! You take stairwell 7i to passage 1z and then..." Stevie rattled off more stairwells and passageways.

Valerius listened to them carefully even as adrenaline poured into his system. Raziel was now completely awake and shifting uneasily. Its claws dug into the earth of its lair. It wanted to get to the White Dragon.

Iolaire is brave. It will take care of Caden, Raziel assured him.

They are goodhearted, Raziel. I do not want them to have to kill...

Raziel's eyes burned redly. It said nothing, but he knew it was intent on the same thing. He also caught a whiff of Raziel's former attitude towards humans, and even other Shifters, which was that they would be better off on a mountaintop with just them, Caden and Iolaire.

Sometimes I feel the same, Valerius admitted.

"Okay, I know which way to go," George told them.

149

"You *best*," Valerius growled.

"This way!" George moved more like a frightened rabbit than a Snake Shifter as he headed left instead of right and up another set of stairs.

Every moment being crushed beneath the mountain in those stinking, twisting tunnels had Valerius' skin twitching. Raziel was pressed against the inside of his chest as if it would break through at any moment. That would be a disaster and both of them knew it. But the dragon within him was almost on top and his eyes burned with crimson fire, which he realized when George happened to glance back at him and jumped three feet up into the air. George ran *faster*, which suited Valerius just fine.

Stevie must have called George again because George put a finger to the bluetooth and asked, "Stevie? What is it?" There was a pause and then, "Seriously? Iolaire is *sniffing* the Faith? No, no, you must be misunderstanding what they're doing."

But Valerius suddenly knew that Stevie was right. Iolaire *was* sniffing the Faith. They were smelling for bombs!

Very clever, Caden! He thought.

His thoughts though did not reach the young man or the White Dragon Spirit. They were too far away or maybe they were both too tense to connect.

"How far?" Valerius barked.

Another fearful glance was sent back towards him. "N-not far! Just down this hallway and then there's a door and you're there and--"

The rest of George's words were lost as Valerius surged forward with Kaila keeping up with him. He raced until he reached the metal and wood bound door. If he had kept up at that speed, he would have burst through the door as if it were made of paper instead of inches of solid wood and metal. But he slowed his forward momentum. He reached for the handle. The door may have been locked--it probably was--but he wrenched it open. There was a scream of metal, but it was overshadowed by the singing. The Faith were singing. Loudly. About the White Dragon.

Valerius pulled up his hood and gestured for Kaila to do the same.

They might have to reveal themselves, but maybe they could somehow keep this under wraps. He stuck his head out of the door. The door was situated at the base of the last set of Stairs. There was a platform that was about one hundred feet long and wide before there were a few more steps into the huge market area.

They were about twenty feet behind the line of dozens of the members of the Faith all lined up with Iolaire's head leaning towards them. In fact, Iolaire was being hugged very fiercely by one of the Faith. Iolaire's eyes were closed and it looked so happy. For a moment, Valerius wondered if he had misunderstood the "sniffing" that Stevie had been talking about. But then the Faith member's hood fell back and she turned her head. Her profile explained everything.

Caden's mother!

The one beside her, Raziel murmured. *I smell...*

Valerius?! Caden's voice blasted in his mind.

Valerius' gaze shot up to Iolaire's head. The White Dragon's gaze was fixed upon him and there was panic in those huge eyes.

Caden--

Bomb! My mom! Beside her! Caden cried, his ability to communicate overwhelmed by fear for his mother.

Valerius' gaze snapped to the person that Raziel had indicated something seemed off about. His heart stutter-stopped in his chest. There was something in the person's right hand. They had curled their hand around what looked like a pen with a button on the end. There looked to be a cord connected to the bottom of this pen-like object that snaked underneath the person's sleeve and was attached to something hidden beneath the voluminous robes.

In less than a second, Valerius knew that there were only so many ways this could go and if they picked the wrong way to stop it then a lot of people were going to die, potentially Caden's mother.

If that was a handheld detonator, all the person needed to do was push the button on the top. An act that would take a second. They would blow up right there and then.

Caden could grab his mother and protect her from the blast but that would mean others would die. Such an act would save Caden's mother, but would wound the young man for the lives lost. He would not be able to forgive himself.

Valerius and Kaila could run out there and each of them take an arm. They could break the person's fingers and stop them from pressing the button if they could get to them before they noticed. But the trigger in the person's hand might not be the only one. Perhaps there was a co-conspirator with them, watching, who could set the bomb off. Or maybe there was a timer that would go off eventually anyways well before a bomb squad could get there.

There was only one way that Valerius saw this working. Caden would have to grab the person and fly them out through the Gash. Valerius and Kaila's Dragons were too big to fit. Only Iolaire could get through. They could fly the person away from any other people and the bomb could be dealt with that way. If they exploded themselves, neither Caden nor Iolaire would be hurt. Not physically anyways.

It is the only way, Raziel growled. *Who is doing this? Who is making these foolish people kill themselves?*

I do not know. But we will find out, Valerius promised the Black Dragon Spirit.

"What if they are not the only one?" Kaila fiercely whispered. "Why send one when you could send two or ten? And not have them be wearing white and sing? They stand out."

She was right. Truthfully, smuggling explosives into the Below *before* the event would have been easier. This person was the only one they'd found, but there could be others mixed in the crowd.

Valerius grunted, "But we can only see one bomber. If either of us starts to look for others--"

"They might see and detonate the bomb?" Kaila nodded. "Perhaps Iolaire can cut off the bomb? It is likely in a vest or--"

"No. We cannot chance it detonating. Iolaire must get them out of here then you and I can start looking for others involved in this," Valerius said, though he knew that it was likely the others--if there were others--would simply detonate themselves.

There's no other choice. Already they are getting suspicious as Caden isn't sniffing anyone any longer.

Indeed, the reporters nearest them started to note that Iolaire was now seemingly as frozen as the ice they'd created on the steps.

A male reporter nervously remarked to his petite female counterpart, "What do you suppose Iolaire is thinking, Janet? I would swear that it looks afraid or alarmed!"

"You're right, Roger. The evident emotion shown by Iolaire with that last member of the Faith has been replaced! I wonder what's wrong?"

The believer with the bomb was *twitching* and looking around surreptitiously. He saw their feet shifting. They were afraid the gig was up. They would race towards the crowd any minute now and end their lives with as many others as they could in the hopes that Spirits would join with the humans. No matter that he wanted to shield Caden, he couldn't.

Just like in everything else...

Valerius, what do we do? They're getting suspicious! Caden's voice was high and tight.

Valerius breathed in deeply. *Caden, you and Iolaire need to snatch the bomber up as fast as you can. Then you need to fly them out of the Below to the open fields far beyond Reach. I'll have a bomb squad meet you out there.*

They'll detonate before then! The horror in Caden's voice was unmistakable. But before Valerius had to say some meaningless soothing words, Caden said himself, *I understand. The only thing that matters is that they don't detonate near anyone else!*

Exactly. Move as fast as you can, Valerius told him. *It won't hurt you or Iolaire if they detonate.*

I know. I'm not worried about that, Caden told him.

Brave boy. Now do it, Caden, Valerius told him.

There was no hesitation. Iolaire's massive right clawed forelimb shot out and snatched the person with the bomb around the middle. Their arms were pinned to their sides, but that didn't mean they couldn't press that trigger. The only hope was that they had dropped the detonator. Then in one fluid movement, Iolaire flexed its legs and was up in the air. The crowd let out confused cries as Iolaire streaked from the Below and was free of the mountain. Valerius let out a breath of relief. They hadn't detonated! Maybe Caden really could keep them from doing so until he got the bomb squad out there.

Valerius turned to George. "Call Captain Simi of the Claw. Tell him to get the bomb squad out to Iolaire. Do you understand?"

George was just beginning to nod when Kaila grabbed his arm. He swung around and realized that there was another member of the Faith who had a detonator in their hand. They were frantically pressing it but nothing was happening. A few white robed members of the Faith were pointing and crying out at them, not clear what they were doing or why, but knowing it was bad. The bomb was not going off though. Something had gone wrong.

Valerius did not think. He moved. He dove towards the figure in white that was still frantically trying to kill themselves and any others that they could take with them. Or maybe they thought that, like Caden, they would be chosen to bond with a Spirit. He would never let that happen.

Valerius grabbed the figure and then turned with them tight against his body as he leaped into the air and shifted. There were screams from the crowd. He saw people trying to scatter as Raziel appeared above them. The member of the Faith was in his right clawed hand, still frantically pressing the detonator. He crushed them to his chest and covered them with both of his powerful forelimbs. He got in one pump of his powerful wings before he felt the bomb go off and the person become splatter in his claws.

Blood and particles of flesh, bone and organs rained down on the crowd below.

FAITHFUL

*I*olaire shot through the Gash like a white arrow and was out into the day. The blue sky and scudding white clouds that were as insubstantial as cotton candy were so welcome after the closed, almost suffocating interior of the Below.

Caden's heart though was pumping not from the exertion of flying or the beauty of the day, but fear. Any moment, the frail and tiny human in his hand could explode and he would be able to do nothing. Even though it would only be one death on his conscience--one that had *chosen* to do this--Caden knew he would be haunted by their death forever. And as a Shifter, forever had a very real meaning now.

Just as they cleared Reach, Caden heard an explosion behind them. They jerked their head around and saw through the Gash the huge form of Raziel inside of the Below. Red "rain" fell down from Raziel onto the crowd. It was blood. It was...

There was another bomber! Caden cried to Iolaire. *Valerius! Raziel! Are they okay?*

Iolaire let out an agitated sound. But then Caden got the image of Iolaire and Raziel touching foreheads. Nearly touching rather. All was fine. Valerius and Raziel could not be hurt by a bomb any more than they could. Even though Caden understood that, intellectually, he still felt sick with worry.

We need to get this one as far away from people as possible, Iolaire!

Iolaire let him glance down at the figure in their right clawed forelimb as they continued to fly. The Faith member's hood was flattened against their face so he couldn't see who they were. But if they were one member of his mom's group, he would recognize them. Hell, he would *know* them personally. His mother had her Faith buddies over for dinners frequently. His only hope was that they had called in others to join them for the day's events. He mentally pleaded for that to be true.

Who is this? Who would be willing to kill themselves and others?

Iolaire made a low soft moan of regret that anyone would take life so easily. The White Dragon Spirit then started to circle a field to land in. They were far from anyone or any structures. They could easily be seen by the bomb unit coming from Reach, but far enough away from anyone that they could easily take off if curious onlookers approached. They would not allow anyone to be hurt if they could help it.

Iolaire softly landed on the tilled field. Their claws dug deep into the rich earth and the scent of living things rose up to their nose. Both of them gazed down at the member of the Faith still clutched in their claws. The person was breathing heavily--actually hyperventilating--and trying to move, but was unable to.

Let's find out who this is, shall we, Iolaire?

Iolaire twittered in agreement. They reached over with their left clawed forelimb and delicately pulled the hood back. Long blond hair covered the Faith member's face. There was a sprinkling of gray in it. But even without seeing her face, Caden recognized her.

Her name was Jennifer Pascal. She was a woman in her mid-fifties who often spoke in a low, whispery voice and had eyes full of zeal when she talked about the wonder of the Spirits. He remembered, specifically, one visit she'd had to his house where she'd encountered a spider and had insisted on carrying it outside instead of smooshing it like his mother had wanted to do.

But here she was.

With a bomb.

Trying to kill *people*.

She looked up at him out of those eyes which were wide again, but this time with fear instead of wonder. He almost relished that. She should be afraid. If she was going to hurt people then she was his enemy! He tilted her back so that he could see the detonator hanging five inches below her fingertips. She must have dropped it which was why she hadn't detonated herself like the one that Valerius had caught.

"White Dragon," she said in that same whispery voice he remembered. The voice she'd used when asking Caden for a second glass of lemonade. "Oh, White Dragon, you are so beautiful. So precious. Yes, you are worth it all."

They shook her with anger and her head snapped back and forth. Frustration filled him as he wanted to shout at her but could not, "WHY? WHY DID YOU DO THIS? WHY WOULD YOU DO THIS?"

He guessed he knew the answer. She hoped that some of the people that were killed would bond with Spirits and be saved. Those that weren't... Well, they didn't matter evidently. There would be more Shifters in the world. It didn't matter how many humans were lost for their gain.

Caden! Valerius called to him.

Iolaire! Raziel cried to the White Dragon Spirit.

Their neck swiveled around to see Valerius shift into the massive Black Dragon just outside of the Gash. Valerius must have shifted back inside the Below, raced out of the Gash, and then shifted again. Both Caden and Iolaire's spirits lifted at seeing them.

"The Black Dragon," Jennifer squeaked and he felt a tremor go through her.

He didn't blame her fear at the sight of Raziel. Seeing the Black Dragon approach was like seeing a fire-breathing locomotive stream down the tracks. Valerius was to them in seconds as Raziel's massive wings sent them through the air like a rocket. They landed nearby, digging deep furrows into the earth as they skidded to a halt. Immediately, Raziel was moving to Iolaire. It pressed its forehead against Iolaire's. It reminded Caden of how mated swans greeted one another. The Dragons gave a deep sigh of pleasure as if it were a relief to touch.

He could feel Raziel's hot breath and the stink of sulfurous fires, which wreathed the Black Dragon's mighty fangs. Iolaire fluttered its wings in pleasure and twittered at Raziel who let out some deep purring sounds from its throat. For a moment, both dragons closed their eyes.

Caden, are you all right? Valerius asked.

I'm fine! What about you? Caden cried. *There was another bomber, wasn't there?*

Not just one. Three. Kaila has caught the other. She will be joining us shortly, Valerius explained.

A third!

Iolaire's eyes opened as they heard another set of wings flapping. Sure enough, Lana was coming towards them. Lana's iridescent aquamarine colored scales made it appear as if part of the Caribbean ocean had taken flight. She landed heavily near them with another Faith member clutched in her left clawed forelimb. Caden was grateful that, like Iolaire, she was small enough to get through the Gash. From the crumbled rocks that still dusted Lana's broad shoulders though, he could see it had been a much tighter fit for them to get through.

The three Dragons regarded one another. Lana's bright yellow-orange eyes sparkled with mirth as she took in the swan-like activities of the Black and White Dragons. He could almost hear Kaila's laughter. Finally, Lana surprised them all by lowering her head to both Iolaire and Raziel. After a moment, Raziel inclined its head curtly.

Iolaire stepped over to Lana and gave a twitter of greeting. Lana lifted its head, eyes widening with surprise and then pleasure, before Lana let out a sound similar to that of a dolphin. More twittering from Iolaire. The two of them were talking though Caden could not understand them. They pressed their cheeks together as if they were old friends. They only moved away from one another when Raziel's massive head lowered to break them apart, evidently jealous.

Did Raziel just have a jealous moment there, Valerius? Caden laughed.

I think so! Valerius sounded amused.

Lana chirps too loudly, Raziel suddenly muttered and there was a slightly embarrassed, affronted tone to its usual grumble.

Oh, right, Raziel. Nice try there! You just want Iolaire all to yourself! Caden told the Black Dragon Spirit.

That just had Caden laughing harder, which he knew was partly from hysteria. Someone had died. So many others nearly had. His mental chuckles quickly faded away.

Caden, I am going to shift back to my human form. I want to start speaking to these people, Valerius told him. *I think in the presence of three Dragons they will be awed into perhaps telling us the truth.*

Right! Is... is my mom okay? I mean--

She's fine, Caden, though like the other Faith members, she is being questioned by the Claw, Valerius said. *Don't worry though. It is a formality. Your mother is one of the few people we can be sure is not behind this.*

Yeah, she'll be devastated to find out that the Faith is behind the bombings. Or, at least, some of them are anyways, Caden stated. *It can't be all of them, right?*

With a grunt of agreement, Valerius shifted once into his human form. Iolaire lowered Jennifer to the ground, though it did not release her, while Lana--realizing what they were up to, did the same. Valerius stalked over to Lana's prisoner and pulled their hood back. Caden let out a gasp, which Valerius heard over their link.

Do you know him, Caden?

I do. His name is Cary Stewart. He's a librarian at Reach University, Caden said as he then told Valerius who Jennifer was as well. He explained everything he knew about them, which admittedly wasn't much.

Looking between the dreamy Jennifer and the studious Cary, Caden had a sense of unreality. Of all the people who he would have suspected, these two would not have been on the list. Both of them were mild mannered. Both were fully committed to the Faith though as well. They worshiped Shifters and spoke of the Spirits in hushed, reverential tones. But still, Caden would never have suspected either of them being willing to kill to bring more Shifters into the world.

I don't understand this, Caden told Valerius. *These guys are really into Shifters and Spirits, but they've always been the type that Spirits have a plan, you know? Like they would never dream of putting their judgment before a Spirit's. Until now...*

I see, Valerius answered as he looked grimly at the owlishly-blinking Cary. The man usually wore glasses but he didn't have them on today and was clearly having trouble focusing on Valerius. *We shall find out.*

"Are there timers on your bombs?" Valerius asked the two prisoners.

Both Cary and Jennifer cringed when Valerius spoke. His voice was arctic and even Caden felt a little like shrinking down, not wanting to have Valerius speak that way to him.

"*Answer me,*" Valerius hissed, leaning in until there was but an inch between his nose and Cary's.

"N-no," Cary gasped out, his voice reedy and thin.

"If you are lying to me," Valerius pointed a finger against his chest, "it will not be just *you* who suffers, but all those you care about!"

Caden didn't believe Valerius would hurt innocents, but his temper was notorious enough that these two believed it.

"There's not! We swear!" Jennifer cried. "It was thought too risky if we were delayed in getting into the Below."

I think they're telling the truth, Valerius, Caden admitted. Though he was haunted by Serai biting a poisoned tooth, these two hadn't attempted to take their lives so far. *What were they promised, Valerius? Why would they do this?*

There were wails from sirens in the far distance as the Claw and the police came to disarm the bombs. Valerius pointed to where the sound was originating from, which was still some distance away.

"That could be the sound of your saviors or your doom." Valerius jerked away the robe to show the vest that Cary wore that was packed with explosives. "Why would you do this?"

"Because it *has* to be done! Don't you know that? Don't you understand?" Cary asked, his face pinked with effort to explain.

"Understand why you would kill yourself and innocents? No, I do not understand," Valerius growled.

"The amount of Shifters being created *must* increase!" Jennifer cried. "And quickly!"

"Why?" Valerius scowled at her.

"Humans destroy everything, especially if it is good," Cary said softly and his head fell forward. Some of his thinning reddish brown hair waved in the breeze.

"Yes, through your *bombs*," Valerius growled.

"No! I mean... *yes*, some will die, but those that *live* are so much more important!" Jennifer tilted her head towards Caden and Iolaire.

Caden swallowed. *Tell her that she's wrong! One White Dragon was not worth all the people who would have died if they had been successful!*

"Iolaire does not agree with you. Iolaire is in pain at what you sought to do," Valerius told Cary and Jennifer.

"We don't want to hurt people, but it's the only way to stop the war that's coming," Cary said.

What war? What is he talking about? Caden demanded to know.

"The only war coming is the one you are starting," Valerius said.

But Cary vigorously shook his head. "Jasper Hawes and Humans First aren't an aberration. They aren't some *fringe* movement. As things get worse and worse for humanity, humanity will do what it does best: destroy that which stands in its way."

"As strong as you all are," Jennifer picked up, "there are simply more humans than there are Shifters. And while the Dragons are immune to bombs and bullets, the other Shifters are not. Humans will call your bluff about what you're willing to do to them in response. Will the Dragons lay waste to the entirety of the world? No. It would make you rulers of nothing."

Cary vigorously nodded his head. "Don't you see? While there will always be those that fear you, desperation will make others ignore that fear and do terrible things. That desperation has been growing and growing. It's coming to a head."

Caden was stunned by their words, but what bothered him--what scared him--was that he could see the logic in them. It was terrible logic. It was utterly desperate. But were they wrong that humanity would rise up against the Shifters? They had 30-years of relative peace, but things were changing as the division between haves and have-nots, or rather the Shifters and humans, became more and more stark.

He thought of his own father's frustration with the way things were. If Caden hadn't become the White Dragon Shifter, his father's role at the firm would have continued to go downhill. His assignments would become less and less. His role circumscribed. He'd told Caden that it was all but decided how many humans would have to be hired. A quota. But no clients wanted humans representing them. Or, at the very least, no human would be the main attorney.

"It takes away hope, Caden," his father had told him. "Before you could aspire to be anything."

"But, Dad, even before there were people who would never be a lawyer, because of the circumstances of their birth and--"

"Yes, that's true, but the amount of people who are now in that position is so much greater," his father answered. "The potential for rising up from where you began was there before. Maybe it was an illusion for some. But now? You can't become a Shifter through hard work. No matter what you do, unless you luck out with becoming a Shifter, you are stuck."

"Well, what do you want Shifters to do about it? I mean, there are more humans than Shifters, but just as many humans want to have the Raven Shifter lawyer instead of the human one or the military packed with Werewolves instead of human soldiers," Caden pointed out with a touch of exasperation. "Humans have a choice about all of that!"

"Yes, they do." His father's shoulders slumped and he ran a hand through his hair. "It's hard to put yourself at a perceived disadvantage. You want the best. We all want the best. But what if the best will never be human? What then?"

What then would be people like Landry going to jail because her brothers' desperation had turned to hatred.

"Do you think that setting bombs and killing people will win people to your cause?" Valerius asked Cary and Jennifer with a shake of his long dark hair.

"We are not trying to win people over," Jennifer said sadly. "We are just doing what must be done. What is the best for everyone. We don't expect to be revered for it, or even understood."

"But you expect to be Shifters because of it, don't you?" Valerius pointed out. His hands went to his hips as he stared hard at both of them. "Tell me you did not!"

"Of course, there is that hope," Cary admitted with a wry smile. "I would so love to be worthy of--"

"Being a Shifter does not make you *worthy!*" Valerius snapped. "Believe me, if good people were the only people who were changed, I would not be here. Many would not be here."

"You have the soul of a warrior, King Valerius. No one expects you to be a saint. That is not your nature," Jennifer told him.

"Why do you think Shifters are better than humans?" Valerius scoffed.

"Shifters may not be better but it is through them that the Spirits get to experience this world." Jennifer looked dreamy. "Tell me that it is not a blessed thing to allow Raziel physical form in this world. Tell me that Raziel does not add something... inexpressibly wonderful to our existence."

Valerius frowned, but said nothing.

She's right about that, Caden said to Valerius.

"There may be Shifters that are not good stewards for all Spirits, but the destruction of one leads to the destruction of both," Cary explained. "They must be protected and the only way to do that is to bring more into our existence. Humanity must be made to see that a war with the Shifters will only lead to its likely decimation. The more Shifters there are, the better the odds."

"Bombs are *not* the answer," Valerius told him with a look of disgust.

"It's not just bombs. You should talk to King Illarion about the suicides in the camps," Jennifer told him. "Speak to King Anwar about the empty villages where people have gone off into the desert to die or come back as Shifters. Ask Queen Kaila here about the drownings. There are more and more. Ask her."

Valerius looked over at Kaila. Lana's eyes had widened as if it was surprised at the Faith member's words, but then a worried expression crossed Lana's face.

Valerius... are they right? Is this happening? Caden heard the panic in his voice and the dread.

I sense I am not the only Dragon who has failed to see everything in his territory, Valerius answered grimly.

"In every territory, the Faithful are doing what they must," Cary said.

"Why kill others? Why not kill yourselves?" Valerius asked.

"Even if every one of the Faithful was to turn into a Shifter--which we do not--it would not be enough to bolster the Shifter ranks to dissuade the violence humans *will* inflict upon them," Jennifer answered simply. "Besides, there must be some who remain behind and spread the word."

Is every member of the Faith a part of this? Caden asked. *I know my mom isn't! I mean... she can't be... can she?*

The sound of sirens and the blue and red flashing lights of the police and Claw were much nearer now. They had left Reach and were racing over the country roads to get there and remove the bombs. Caden feared what would happen if the vests could not be successfully removed.

"You will tell me the names of everyone involved in this plot!" Valerius snapped as if he realized that their chances to get more information would fade once the Claw got there.

"We don't know," Jennifer said. "I was not even aware that Cary was one of us before now."

So... sleeper cells? That's what they're called right? Caden asked.

Yes, that would be the name for it, Valerius agreed.

"So we need to imprison every member of the Faith then?" Valerius crossed his arms over his chest.

"You can't," Jennifer replied. She was not defensive. She was not terrified at the prospect. It was just a simple statement of fact.

"Oh? Why not?" Valerius asked.

"Because you'll never be able to identify us all. Many don't even come to the prayer groups. Most don't wear white. And the word will spread far and wide if you persecute the Faith," Jennifer answered. "Even today's failed plan will have the benefit of drawing in new believers as whispers of the truth get out."

Valerius leaned in towards Jennifer. "I assure you that *no one* will know of this insane plan you have. No one will hear from either of you again. There will be no trial. No lawyers. No statements. Nothing. You will simply disappear."

Alarm appeared on Cary's face for a moment. "You can't do that!"

"Of course, I can," Valerius told him with a coldness that was chilling to hear. "You are already gone. You just don't know it yet."

The wail of sirens was deafening as the police vehicles screeched to a halt fifty feet from them.

"King Valerius, you can't stop this," Jennifer said with head held high.

"We're doing what's best for Shifters and humanity," Cary added, also looking serene.

Valerius stared at them both. "The Faithful do not rule this world. The Dragons do. And we will stop you."

Story Continues in Book 6!

Listen to Dragon's Reign!

Dragon's Reign is also available in audio.

You can find the audiobook at our shop.

Made in the USA
Middletown, DE
07 June 2025